Indivisible

Fanny Howe

SEMIOTEXT(E) • NATIVE AGENTS

ISBN: 1-58435-009-1

Semiotext(e) Editorial:
2571 W. Fifth Street
Los Angeles, Ca. 90057

Semiotext(e) Distribution:
Fax: 213.487.5204
email: nativeagent@earthlink.net

We gratefully acknowledge financial assistance in the publication
of this book from the California State Arts Council.

Design: TK
Illustrations: Peter Kim
Back Cover Photo: Susan Moon

distributed by: The MIT Press, Cambridge, Mass, and London, England

TABLE OF CONTENTS

IN THE WHITE WINTER SUN

1-0

I locked my husband in a closet one fine winter morning.
It was not a large modern closet, but a little stuffy one in a
century old brick building. Inside that space with him were
two pairs of shoes, a warm coat, a chamber pot, a bottle of
water, peanut butter and a box of crackers. The lock was
strong but the keyhole was the kind you can both peek
through and pick. We had already looked simultaneously,
our eyes darkening to the point of blindness as they fastened
on each other, separated by only two inches of wood. Now
I would not want to try peeking again. My eyes meeting his
eyes was more disturbing than the naked encounter of our
two whole faces in the light of day. It reminded me that no
one knew what I had done except for the person I had done
it with. And you God.

1-1

A gold and oily sun lay on the city three days later.
Remember how coldly it shone on the faces of the blind
children. They stayed on that stoop where the beam fell the
warmest. I wasn't alone. My religious friend came up
behind me and put his arm across my shoulder.
"We have to say goodbye," he murmured.
I meant to say, "Now?" but said, "No."
I had seen I'm *nobody* written on my ceiling only that
morning.

Brick extended on either side. The river lay at the end. Its
opposite bank showed a trail of leafless trees. My friend was
tall, aristocratic in his gestures – that is, without greed. He
said the holy spirit was everywhere if you paid attention.
Not as a rewarded prayer but as an atmosphere that threw
your body wide open. I said I hoped this was true. He was
very intelligent and well-read. He had sacrificed intimacy
and replaced it with intuition.

I wanted badly to believe like him that the air is a conscious
spirit. But my paranoia was suffusing the atmosphere, and
each passing person wore a steely aura. "Please God don't
let it snow when I have to fly," he said and slipped away. My
womanly body, heavy once productive, and the van for the
children, gunning its engine, seemed to be pounded into
one object. It was Dublin and it wasn't. That is, the Irish
were all around in shops and restaurants, their voices too
soft for the raw American air and a haunt to me. "Come on.

Let's walk and say goodbye," he insisted. We walked towards
St. John the Evangelist.

"I've got to make a confession," I told him. "Can't I just
make it to you? I mean, you're almost a monk, for God's
sake."
"No," said Tom. "The priest will hear you. Go on."
Obediently I went inside. The old priest was not a Catholic.
He was as white as a lightbulb and as smooth. His fingers
tapered to pointed tips as if he wore a lizard's lacy gloves.
It was cold inside his room. Outside – the river brown and
slow. A draft came under the door.

I think he knew that a dread of Catholicism was one reason
I was there. He kept muttering about Rome, and how it
wouldn't tolerate what he would, as an Anglican.

Personally I think pride is a sin. But I said "a failure of
charity" was my reason for being there. This was not an
honest confession, but close enough. The priest told me to
pray for people who bothered me, using their given name
when I did. He said a name was assigned to a person before
birth, and therefore the human name was sacred. Then he
blessed me. Walking out, I felt I was dragging my skeleton
like a pack of branches. After all, a skeleton doesn't clack
inside the skin, but is more like wood torn from a tree and
wrapped in cloth.

Outside Tom was waiting and we walked over the snow. "I
missed that flute of flame that burns between Arjuna and

Krishna — the golden faces of Buddha, and Yogananda, Ramakrishna, Milarepa, and the dark eyes of Edith Stein and Saint Teresa. Are all Americans Protestant? The church was cold, austere. I'm a bad Catholic."

He nodded vaguely and said: "But you're a good atheist. Catholicism has an enflamed vocabulary, don't worry. You can transform each day into a sacrament by taking the eucharist. You just don't want to bother."

Even the will to raise and move a collection of bones can seem heroic. Only an object on one side — or a person — can draw it forwards — or on another side an imagined object or person. Maybe the will responds to nearby objects and thoughts the way a clam opens when it's tapped. "Mechanistic.... We really should put more trust in the plain surface of our actions," I said.
"Do we really have to say goodbye? And leave each other in such a state?"
"We do."
"But first, Tom — I have one favor to ask you."

1-2

Exactly ten years before, during a premature blizzard, I left all my children at home and went to meet my best friends in the Hotel Commander. I did so carrying the weight of my husband like a tree on my back. This was a meeting I couldn't miss, no matter how low I stooped.

The walk from the subway to the hotel was bitter, wet and shiny. Traffic lights moved slowly on my right, while the brick walls and cold gray trees sopped up the gathering snow. I kept my eyes fixed on the left where dark areas behind shrubs and gates could conceal a man, and stepped up my pace.

Lewis and Libby were already seated in a booth in a downstairs lounge. I shook off my coat and sat beside Libby and we all ordered stiff drinks, recalling drunker meetings from earlier youth. I leaned back and kept my eyes on the door, in case my husband appeared and caught me off-guard.

"Relax, Henny," Lewis reproved me.

"I've never met him," Libby cried. "It's unbelievable."

"He's unbelievable," said Lewis.

"He can't be that bad."

"He is. He should be eliminated. He won't let her out of the house, without her lying. She probably said she had a neighborhood meeting tonight. Right?"

"Henny's not a coward."

"She likes to keep the peace though. That's not good."

"I'm going to be back in the spring. I'll meet him then," Libby said. "And if he's all that bad, I will do something to him."

"Henny has an mercenary army of children around her, protecting her against him," Lewis explained. "They aren't even her own."

"Hen, tell me the truth. Do you wish he would die? I'll make him leave you if you want me to," said Libby.

A renunciatory rush went down my spine when I saw, out in the lobby, the back of a man in a pea-jacket and woolen cap. Gathered over, I left the table for the rest room, and Libby followed breathless. She was wringing her hands, smelling of musk rose, and dancing on her pin-thin legs in high heel boots that had rings of wet fur around the tops while I sat in the sink. "Was it him? Was it him?"

We never found out.

That was the same night we climbed out the hotel kitchen window and walked up a slippery hill, one on each side of Lewis, hugging to his arms, while the snow whipped against our cheeks and lips, and we talked about group suicide.

"Phenobarbital, vodka and applesauce, I think."
"No, Kool-aid, anything sweet."
"For some reason."
"Jam a little smear of strawberry on the tongue."
"Or honey."
"Catbirds and the smell of jasmine and we all lie in a line under the stars."
"With great dignity."
"Despite the shitting." "And die." "Die out."
"I can dig it," said Lewis. "I can dig it."
"But we have to do it all together," Libby said.

1-3

There is a kind of story, God, that glides along under everything else that is happening, and this kind of story only jumps out into the light like a silver fish when it wants to see where it lives in relation to everything else.

Snow is a pattern in this story. It was snowing the day of my first visit to the Federal Penitentiary. The ground was strung with pearly bulbs of ice. I had visited many social service offices in my day, but never a prison. I associated prison with sequence and looked around for a way to break out. As a first-time visitor, and in the early moments, I remembered nervously standing with a crowd of strangers waiting for someone familiar to emerge from behind a green door with a big light over it. For each one of us, the familiar person would be a different person, but our experience would be the same. I already know that some conflicts in life have no resolution and have to be treated in a different way from common problems.

But prison seemed to relate to issues of privacy in ways that were unimaginable to those who had never been forcibly hidden. Simplistically I was scared of being in a jail because it was a space that was unsafe from itself, the way a mind is. But I forced myself, as I sometimes do, to go to the place I dreaded the most — to the place that was so repugnant, it could only change me. Maybe the sacred grove of our time is either the prison or the grave site of a massacre. I have always believed I must visit those sacred groves, and not the woodlands, if I want to know the truth. In this case, I only wanted to see someone I loved and to comfort her by my coming. And surely enough, I did undergo a kind of conversion through my encounters with the persons there. When you visit someone in prison, this paranoid question comes up: Do I exist only in fear? The spirit hates cowards. It broods heavily in the presence of fear. I only felt as safe as a baby when I was holding a baby or a child and so, sitting empty-armed, in a roomful of strangers, watching the light over the heavy door, was a test of will.

Then I saw a child — a little boy in the room with me — he was like a leaf blowing across an indoor floor. And while waiting for my friend to come out the door, I moved near him.

I asked him what book he had brought with him. He kept his face down and said, "Gnomes."
"Do you read it yourself, honey?"
"No, I can't. Tom reads it to me."
"Do you want me to read some?"
"Sure," he said and lifted his smile. His eyelids were brown and deeply circled and closed, as long as the eyelids of the dead whose lashes are strangely punctuated by shadows longer than when they were alive and batting. He wore a limpid smile that inscribed a pretty dimple in his right cheek.

"I'm getting obsessed," he said, "with books about gnomes, goblins, elves, hobbits."

"How do you mean obsessed?"

"I want to know everything about them. And sometimes I'm sure they really exist and run around my feet."

"How can you tell?"

"My shoelaces come untied sometimes, and I think I feel them on my shoes."

"I don't know, honey. I've never seen one. Let's go read about gnomes."

When I took his hot little hand in mine, I felt the material charge of will and spirit return to me. I had an instinctual feeling that the room held me fast by my fate. To be here was to be physically "inside" but the way a ghost is inside the world when it returns to haunt someone and still can depart at will. The ghost is confused, paralyzed by its guilt at being present without paying the price for it. Punishment is easily confused with safety.

1-4

There are sequences of sounds that musicians arrange by twelves, repeating the same twelve notes but in alternating and random sequences. They themselves don't know which three or four notes will come out close, in relation to each other.

It is sort of as if someone I loved indicated that he loved me too, but in unexpected moments and ways. And the three words "I love you" only popped into place once, by mistake, and after he had died, as in "too late". There were

no witnesses to our relationship, and this created a
credibility gap. I didn't trust that the experience that he and
I had had had actually taken place because there were no
witnesses; the verb tense was queer. No conventions stuck.
I was the missing person at the graveside ceremony – an
eyeball behind a bush. The person I loved would say "me…
too… you," and this would be months after he died. Would
anyone believe that I just heard him say it, no?

1-5

It was in that prison that I met a religious man for the
second time in my life. Almost every time I visited there the
small boy was there too with his beautiful ringed eyes,
serious long face, and this man beside him. The child often
wore a strange sidelong smile, the way the blind do. I could
tell that his guardian was weirdly unlike a blood father. He
always brought along a book that the boy ran his hand over.
This man was either distracted or brooding when he talked
to the boy's mother, a prisoner who was tiny and wild-
haired and dressed in a green uniform which was fitted to
say "not my own."

They talked about the boy, eyeing him simultaneously. The
mother's expression was sad and inverted. Her eyes pulled
their surroundings inside, and then didn't let them out
again. This was a common expression on many prisoners'
faces here. Many of the women were locked up for drug
crimes. Either they were users or else they lived with a
dealer and took the rap for him. I found out all about this

in upcoming visits. My friend, who had been framed, told me the stories of the prisoners around us. Often the guy was free while his girlfriend and/or mother of his child was locked up for her unwillingness to speak his name to the Feds. Already I knew from experience how quickly a woman's children could end up in foster care if there was no functioning family person. I assumed that this was the case with those three. The man might be a foster father, or a friend. Or was he her boyfriend? I was pretty sure maybe the woman was one of those people who were political prisoners left over from the sixties and seventies. In any case, I concluded there should be a whole separate set of laws for women and watched the boy back onto his mother's lap. Her name was Gemma. One day before jail the man told me about Gemma the prisoner and how he knew her. We stood in puddles that looked like mirrors of shadows around our feet.

"I used to work for a small legal aid firm in Boston," he told me. "I hated law already by then. But a friend called me asking me to defend this woman. She had been part of a bank heist with the Weather Underground. I told him I'd never been in court before, but he persuaded me, and I did it. And failed. Lost. She got forty years. Life, basically."

"And her child?" I asked him. "She was pregnant with him when she went in. It was before they had any maternity programs in prison. She and the kid never really bonded. I have watched out for him ever since. You know. Made sure he had a home."

"What about the father?" was the natural question I asked.
"Never mind, nothing. He couldn't."
"Why? Was he in hiding too?"
"Right, but they are friends. Sort of."
I pressed him: "Why is the child blind? How?"
"She tried to kill herself. With some poison."
"After the trial?"
"During."

We walked from the parking lot towards the prison. I then had a vision of this man having huge lies inside of him, lies like helium that swelled up his spirit until it almost exploded.

I was sure now that he was the father. "What's your name?" I asked with a squint as if I had only forgotten it.
"Tom," he said pleasantly. "I'm in preparation for entering a monastery. What's yours?"

The sun seemed to be setting at two p.m. It shriveled and paled like a coin dropped into still yellow milk.

Inside the checking area I handed over my wallet and keys and found my tongue loosened. I am known for my silence, and liked for it, but with Tom I could talk. "I'm used to seeing the children, not the mothers, when they are lost, separated," I told him.
"I see the beginnings of their lives, not the conclusions, as in this case."
"What do you mean?"

"I'm a foster mother – or was – I took children home."
"That's interesting. Want to go for a walk later?"

Outside again, Tom and I went for our first walk. It was
early spring when the forsythia branches were yellowing up
for the arrival of their flowers. The reservoir was scalloped
behind a chain-link fence. The air was between black and
oyster. He told me he was going back to Canada ultimately.
He was going to live as a monastic in a Benedictine
community. "Why wait?" I asked.
"To get the boy settled. I can't leave until he has a home."
"That could take awhile, because of his age, and affliction."
"Maybe, maybe not…. but I would love to be somewhere
warmer than this."
"Me too." There was a tolerant if melancholy quality to him
that eased me. My breathing slowed, I believed I could
express myself well in words, and nothing bad would
happen. He seemed desireless, without being cold and
ironic. I already dreaded saying goodbye although that word
was planted and fated, because of his stated plans. On many
of our walks, no words in fact passed between us. As soon
as I had no fear of speaking to him, I had nothing much to
say. It was in this silence that we grew familiar enough to
travel side by side.

1-6

In a matter of weeks we agreed to go to the border of
Mexico. The boy stayed behind with his foster family. It was
late April, 1997. We went there because this border

represented the most repulsive cut on the continent. A festering trench. By mutual agreement we decided to plant ourselves in that alien landscape; to carry a mystifying revulsion to its limits. This was a test of faith for both of us. He was still uncertain about entering a religious community. In retrospect I see that he had several months of exclaustrated wandering ahead of him. He wanted to know how much isolation he could stand. I wanted to learn about pressure without interference. He wanted to persuade me to become the caretaker of the blind child; I wanted to show him how much my freedom meant to me. So we had paused, together, there in an abandoned household on a canyon where it only rained after Christmas. Sand, dust, small stones, loose canyons emitting the gas of past massacres. The huts were wooden, open to spiders, snakes, lizards, birds and illegal aliens who fled like deer at our approach. Now when a fog dulled the difference between mother earth and air, we both remembered snow, our natural northern habitat. Tom said that Southern California was like a body without a head. "One of those bodies they plan to grow for body parts, to harvest, so to speak." Not far from our desert retreat lay miles and miles of condominium settlements splashed with blue pools. I was sewing curtains. The windowpanes held thick wadded spider webs and the bodies of flies and bees dried in them as if the webs were silver hammocks. At home I heard it was snowing again – large wet cloud-shavings.

1-7

Home for me then was on the edge of Boston in a town abutting Roxbury and Franklin Park. The pit and the puddingstone. Old Victorian mansions were shaded by spectacular trees which were pollinated by Olmsted's landscaping ventures around town. The streets had a secretive drift. Cardinals, bluejays, sparrows, swallows, crickets, robins and crows shivered the leaves with their singing. Almost every person was poor or about to be. You had to leave if you were getting money, because the neighborhood could not tolerate inequalities. Old families, all of them Irish, Puerto Rican or Black clung to their two-and-three families while the newly arrived (soon to leave) dwelled in single family houses they renovated and converted into apartments before departure. My old house had not been renovated, but needed a new roof and a coat of paint, not much to make its butter yellow facade look permanent where it hid its flaws behind a mound of granite and five varieties of evergreen. It was occupied as usual by transients who sent me the rent for their rooms. McCool my husband was not allowed, by the courts, to pass the gate and enter, but when I was away the tenants called him anyway if a rat was swimming in the toilet bowl or a bat was sleeping in the shower. He would then enter our house proudly with his toolbox, look slowly around the premises he once occupied, deal with the problem and then postpone leaving over a cup of tea and chit-chat.

McCool said his dark hair and complexion were a result of the wreck of the Spanish Armada on the west coast of Ireland. The word "wreck" clung to his features then, like weeds on stones. McCool was not his given name, but his singing name. He played Celtic tunes with a small band who toured during March, and he played solo in Boston pubs the rest of the time. McCool and I had some qualities in common. We were both what they call the working poor. We were unrewarded artists – he on his fiddle played since boyhood, and me in my films which were obscure meditations on seven themes:

1. geographic cures as religious acts
2. parental betrayals and lies
3. the nearly unsupportable weight of the world's beauty (God)
4. how to stay uncorrupted
5. a political act as a gesture of existential discomfort
6. childhood for children
7. race in America

These themes found their forms in my dreams and I committed them first to paper in the dark morning hours where eastern clouds were inscribed on our greasy kitchen windows. I wanted to find the unifying idea behind these themes, one sequence of lights that would illuminate the situation. Meanwhile McCool's music was never recorded but he moved from one shabby venue to the next, playing melodies that were both traditional and new ones he had composed. He was too early and too late for the Irish music scene. He was good at it, but got lost carrying it somewhere. He told stories. He lied. He had no conscience but compensated for this lack with a dogged survivalist creed. He would stay around, no matter what, and be difficult for everyone. To be a problem, he said, was the credo of his revolution. He needed someone to copy, rather than someone to love, and he was as faithful as a wolf in his way, never ceasing to pursue his family or stay near, no matter what the law said. Everyone knows someone like him.

A total of twelve children passed through our house. Nine of them were temporary; two returned twice, then left again; three were siblings; two were sexually abused, four were beaten; three had ammunition and drugs in their homes; one was abandoned on a church step; two had been left to stepfathers who didn't want them; one was autistic. Three children arrived as toddlers and stayed for life. These were the twins, and little Dorothy who helped me. She was motherly but became a nun in Yogananda's Self-Realization Fellowship after doing foreign missionary work. The twins also traveled far, separately. Then they returned and settled near their childhood home, my house. They both have done well in the world. I didn't adopt any of them and they could call me whatever they wanted. I didn't want to pretend they were my natural-born children but to use the slave model—a situation where abandoned children were simply taken in. They called their caretakers Aunt or Cousin. This way no one tampered with the actual source of their existence, or set up a potentially disappointing arrangement. Strangely my three did call me Ma, Mummy and Mom, though they referred to me as Henny. They always called McCool McCool because it was cool. These three became used to an adult man being an outsider. They were street-wise kids who went through the national busing crisis siding with the black students and staying involved with race from kindergarten on.

Later I guess they chose to be permanently engaged with that most absurd social issue because its very absurdity liberated them from all other delusions. These children were my soldiers. They liked to have fun. They grew up in that old house, watching other babies come and go, and left when they were eighteen. They themselves arrived as inert beings, barely able to whine or lift their heads, so neglected they made solitude into a luxury. Contact gradually restored them.

But when their training was over, and they left home, I could barely remember a single act of parenting. Instead I manned the everyday hassles without the bending over, but weeping out of the same personal problem. It was in my misty maternalist past that the life of the spirit developed into its present form. Material flotilla floated away, even the thoughts I had about children, and became transparencies. The passages, acts, encounters, always in transit and irritating made me move as a mother crab back and forth, sideways through the rooms, tipping and lifting the faces of whole tiny faces up to mine. And these faces changed continually becoming new faces and all of them were attached to the hands they would identify as their own for life. Home tried to stay stationary, to keep them tied, returning to their rooms and views of the moon, but once they were gone, they were really gone, and I was just a mourner at a vast immaterial site.

THROUGH THE EYES OF THE OTHER

2-1

It is now many months after that first prison visit – again snow dots the night sky. A blue moon in late February will follow these white nights, there will be a thaw, a gush, this chunk of earth cutting up into cascades of fluid and sex. It is the copper light that I see on the water that saves me.

A net is like a honeycomb with its ridges and holes. But a net is not sticky, its weaving is made of string and air. I believe there are many similar geometries making up the physical world, but we can't see them. Something is wrong because there are emotions between people a few miles apart. You would think that the dead had just traveled somewhere else material.

The details of streets along and near the river emerge sometimes and often against the meow of an ambulance rushing to a hospital nearby. This building is called Terminal Arms by laughing residents. Many of the tenants are elderly on a one-way corridor to the cemetery. The pale green louvered doors beside each entrance to each apartment, and the small wooden polished elevator make it feel like the Paris of my imagination. I hear from two walls in my bedroom and the ceiling the sound of tenants peeing and flushing their old age.

If you make a negative out of the popular image of Jesus' face, you see a set of heart-shaped stains where his skin should be lighted. The sacred heart, flat on his chest, pink with gold sticks coming out of its circumference, looks as if it has fallen from an area of his face where there is usually the beard.

"My guru is within my heart, he is the viveka within my heart," wrote Jnaneshwari. This means to me that our hearts are our whole bodies and our wounds are visible.

There are factories that produce the faces of Jesus and Mary out of one mold and press the beard onto only one of them.

Snow clings to the rough brick walls and interferes with my view of the street and the river. People walking dogs, heads bowed, pass, and even in this weather there are joggers who in their spanking suits look like silhouettes from old children's books—the Pied Piper, say, leaping and stretching evilly along the page's border. Almost everywhere I look my eyes are straining against my guilt... rising and leaving the shadows. Silence is incorruptible as long as its body is not possessed by anyone else.

The minute it becomes property, even its silence seems rooted in treachery.

I was fascinated by her – by them – as I waited there in the prison each day. It was as if I could read them into my future, like hills on a horizon towards which I was inexorably moving. The man was dark and handsome in a warm tormented way. But I wondered if he was half-blind. He never looked at the woman but always down while his hand on the boy s shoulder was heavy. The blind boy would lead him around the chairs and tables while the woman watched. She was like a small animal, who might have padded feet and claws, her eyes wary under long lids, her cheekbones high, her body quickly gesturing, and withdrawing. I could tell that all access to happiness was closed off in her.

2-2

In the apartment the heat goes on as soon as the sun is gone. The pipes bang and chirp as if a family of crickets is dancing up a storm. The view to the river covers about one hundred yards. There is a well-used road between, a riverbank, the river, another riverbank, another road, and more roads beyond that one, but also hills and tops of buildings. The window is facing northwest. To the left the river is sucked in to the sea or disgorged. Still I do get a sunset and a sunrise along those lines of bank and river and the bricks turn into gold. My husband remains locked in the closet where he makes a racket. I don't want to tell anyone that he is there, least of all the monkish Tom, because everyone believes that a person is obligated by witnessing an event to report it. But if you're just standing peacefully by, then are you responsible for a glance to the side at something you knew would happen sooner or later. I mean, if you dreamed the thing would happen and then you are there finally, watching, when it does happen, are you responsible? Are you in a way the instigator? The most confusing situation is to be a ghost who sees terrible things and can't report it. Sometimes I think that God witnesses events sideways and doesn't stop because it all goes by so fast, and God can't believe what God just saw. So it is important to tell you everything, God.

2-3

Lewis became a solid man, thick with some belly not really fat because it was tight like a drumskin girdling him. Burly is a better word. He had long eyes with soft eyelids and very thin eyebrows. His phenomenal strength was in his upper torso because of turning those wheels by hand. He didn't laugh now.

"Do you know someone who died, I mean well?"

"Yes, my father," I barely audibly said.

"Wait a minute. How did he die?"

"In Korea."

"Oh right. Poor bastard."

"I'm still waiting for him to come home."

"I believe it. I believe it."

"Believe what."

"That you're waiting like that," he remarked. "You've always acted like someone who had to be somewhere else, just in case. Where to be when he comes, is the question."

"Do you think that a person can use intimacy as a form of resistance? I mean, since you melt into the shape of your enemy...." I asked him.

"Who knows? You mean all your children?" he asked. "All I know is that if there's a God, he eats everything in sight, and women like you keep producing food for him, in the form of children. Why."

"Our babies? Our selves? Him? You must mean It."

"Okay. It. You keep producing bodies for It. Why?"

"I am studying resistance now, Lewis," I said.

"Okay, Henrietta, okay."

He rarely listened to me because I spoke so softly. He would hear and vaguely respond, but really his attention was always elsewhere. Today, war. He told me now that the practice of sacrifice went way back to creation stories where the universe was seen as a giant human – the Purusha – with human attributes. Sacrificing people was a way of offering bodies to the big body of the cosmos itself. Spring was butter to its lips and its lips were butter. Earth goddesses were appeased by the sacrifice of young males because they wanted their seed for more young males and crops. Pentheus, a killjoy who wanted to stop his mother from having fun at night, was ripped apart by his mother herself. She held up his penis triumphantly for everyone to see, even as he screamed Mother it's me! And he listed the legendary wicked women – Cybele, Ma, Dindymene, Hecate, Artemis, Nemesis, Demeter, Baubo, Medusa, Persephone, Isis, Aphrodite, Kali, Durga, Nana, Ishtar, Astarte, Nina of Ninevah, Parvati and the Great Mother – never pausing to wonder what their points of view might be.

"Sacrifice," he concluded, "was the most developed form of materialism – way beyond the ones we know now – it was seeing and being food simultaneously. I think that's why so many women were involved." Loops of tempura glistened on his fork.

"What?" I asked.

We had many dinners together. Usually in the Tokyo Restaurant on a thoroughfare outside the city. Easy for Lewis to park there and undo his chair on the street. We rolled to the same table in a back room almost every time. The impersonal manners of the waiters pleased us both; they never acknowledged having seen us before. He liked one bottle of Kiran beer. I once had a glass of white wine that tasted like water in a graveyard and sent a chill down my spine. Afterwards I only drank saki. Then he had his chicken tempura and I ate a California roll.

We were always at ease together there. It was like being in bed being anywhere with him. The world outside grew cold. We had nothing we wanted but the time that we had.

I could see in his thick aging features the boy I once knew. He could see in mine the girl he met when I was seventeen.

2-4

I had met Lewis at the house of my best friend Libby in April, 1967. He was sprawled on a staircase with some friends, the first black American youth and the most brilliant man almost anyone there had met. It was the North. He was very smooth and hairless and the color of caramel. He never lacked confidence but dared to laugh with his eyes closed. He was twenty two, from the Midwest, a recent Freedom Rider. They had all come up from Mississippi. I listened to him talk about it.

"At one point I was speeding – I mean speeding – in this car with two Northern lawyers, from Oxford to Jackson, Miss., they were drafting documents in long-hand, going to try a case, get some so-called Negroes out of jail, and we got shot at and all of us couldn't believe it, laughed, these mangy dogs running away from the blast while our car shot up dust. That's when I decided to go to law school. That's when it happened."

I hated being so sure so fast but I knew that he was the one I was assigned to cherish.

He talked to white people without wanting to know them. I loved his attitude because I was scared of white grown-ups.

Seventeen, a virgin, a novice in issues of race and sex, I had already been told by one white man, the school principal, that he wouldn't recommend me for any colleges, and I had been kicked out of a courtroom in Downtown Boston where state officials were accusing other white men of being communist. The white firemen shot me down the outside steps with their hoses, only enraging me further, but Lewis held me back. I was a communist sympathizer, as was Lewis who nonetheless believed that the battle between rich and poor had been lost and the poor would always be with us. From the beginning he held the tragic position that the only revolution was the eternal revolution – an inexhaustible struggle for something already lost.

"Is it correct, the way people do, to depend on history to be the judge?" he might ask, and answer: "The idea is that history sorts things out later, in favor of the good and the just. History is the future glutted with recollected facts. It crosses back and forth, making swift but morally astute decisions about who deserves to be famous and who doesn't or didn't. History like God has an ethical bent so people should be nervous about its judgment later on, although to be remembered badly is better than to be forgotten entirely if you are someone who wants to be famous–as opposed to saved."

2-5

I never sat on Lewis's lap. Once he pinned me down across him and I said I would call the police, it was a joke, but he was definitely manhandling me. Gracefulness of gesture had gone from him since he was shot overseas. What radiated out now was not so physical but more like a force-field, it was still attractive. To me. It was not easy loving someone both rejecting and kind. His suffering was so great it rolled up everything else he was feeling like jam inside a sponge cake. He, like so many injured people, seemed to have been chosen to be wounded as a sacrifice for the rest of us. To some his condition indicated bad karma. To others, it was moral ecology that someone had to pay for everyone else's fun and freedom. Besides, he had been cocky. And to still others, it was just an accident made of causes and contingencies. That big power-shouldered man, with light brown skin and a beard to his ears, was often seen laughing at things, papers, people, all by himself. In company he was grumpy.

He could make that wheelchair tip and spin and climb up steps; he moved it as if it was part of his body. But no one with eyes could fail to see what it cost him. Likewise the Hasidic men inside their beards and hats also seemed to be living compensations for the furious freedom of others. And like people who know that they have made choices their faces are hard, not curious or perplexed. Jesus with his curly black beard and prayer shawl might have been like one of them.

"Rabbi, teacher."

"What? What do you want?" Jesus asked.

"Rabbi," they said to him. "Where are you staying?"

"Come and see."

It was about four in the afternoon.

Already it is growing dark. The clouds pour up from the horizon to gorge on the sun going down. Yellow is the first night-cloud warning for snow but it also is the first sign of morning. "Give me what you know, my Lord. Give me that water."

A CRACKLE OF STATIC

¶ 1

Originally the New England native inhabitant was described as out-nosed, black-haired, small-waisted, lank-bellied, with small feet. They were called Brownettoes. Their backs were erect. They ate strawberry, raspberry, cherry, blueberry and elderberry breads. Boiled chestnuts. Crushed butternuts and beechnuts for the bread. They would pound the corn fine, sift it, water it into a dough and pat it into little cakes and bake it on the hot ashes. Raccoon fat for butter or sometimes bear oil. Libby's father was a scholar of life in New England before the Puritans and Pilgrims arrived. He knew everything about weaving, arrowheads, sweat lodges and pottery, long before it was fashionable in the academic world. He worked for a musem instead of a university and felt bitterness all his life. His daughters were supposed to go to an Ivy League college and they did.

I was the well-read daughter of Libby's family maid. Often I had to be hidden with the intensity of our friendship concealed from others. Libby's older sister Eugenia didn't think it was a good idea for Libby to be so close to someone from a lower class. By a stroke of fortune, I was able to attend the same school as them. But I didn't go to the school dances in order to avoid being rejected by anyone, especially Libby who might be embarrassed by me. From our earliest days together, I felt that she had arrived first at every place we visited, that every situation belonged to her, and therefore that she deserved to have whatever she wanted at any given place. This is how deeply the feeling of being second sinks in. I had such a fear of taking exams and doing better than Libby could, I failed them all.

However, it was at Libby's house, before we graduated from high school, that I met the love of my life and could put my failure to good use. I was invited to a party, which included Eugenia and lots of her older friends, in order to celebrate Libby's admission to a top college. It was a day just warm enough to allow the party to spill out and over into their garden. My mother had left the house clean and another maid was there doing the food. I was humiliated at being the only girl we knew in school who was not going to college. But I believe I knew I would get my revenge later, through reading and bold living. Like Dorothea in *Middlemarch* I would learn the price of everything.

3-2

There are very few trustworthy men, much fewer trustworthy teachers, and even fewer holy people in this world. I've never met one outside of a baby or someone about to die. Why are some people born always wanting to be loved when it is so clear that few dare be wholehearted in love. The indifference of others, as well as oneself, should liberate every person to do as he or she pleases all the time. If I could really decide to make this my best year ever, would I know what choices to make – about my job first, since it determines my ability to live at all? No, because I have too much fear or too little desire. "We should all just try to be happy, which is very hard to do," Libby told me.

"Humans by now hate themselves."

She looked at me with her eyebrows raised, lips pursed and then shot forward into an imitation of a laughing Buddha. Her narrow back was always held straight as if she had been trained as a dancer, and she folded her thin cold arms across her stomach pretending to be round and raucous. She was in that final saint-stage. She was bald. Her shirt was saffron colored to match her soul. She was a somewhat indigenous girl – Shawmut from Boston, you could place her in feathers on a green mountain facing the west, one leg resting on a stone. From the movies we learned that white outlaws ruled and exploited the Indians. There was however a happy twist to being a loser that qualified as a form of resistance. Otherwise, why did we side with them every time? "Desiring true freedom, I surrender, I take refuge," is written in the Svetasvatara Upanishad.

Libby Camp was my first friend and sister. Psychics have told me I was her mother in earlier lives. They have also told me I have been a mother enough times in earlier lives and now can move on to a new form.... perhaps to become a nun in an ashram. Libby was the child of two white people. Her father's family, however, began in the New England forests. He interfered with Libby when she was pre-pubescent. I didn't know how bad it was because my intuitions about his evil kept me out of their house while my mother worked inside.

Libby had a horrible life. Alcohol, drugs, unhappy love

affairs and an unrelenting quest for God who seemed to elude her even when she was dying because she was good enough to lack certainty. She had meditated dutifully for years. This discipline made it possible for her to receive without screams all the medieval torments of modern medicine – catheters, bags, chest and brain shunts, tubes down the nose and throat and IVs taped to bruised blood sites, hemorrhoids, enemas, etc. She sat tiny and brown and nutty in her face-making mood, the hospital comedian. Her resistance was always like this – a splitting and scattering of attributes. Together we pretended we were everyone else. For years she had talked solemnly about God but it was a dope-dream and now she admitted that she didn't ever know if God was "just an illusion." As you careen into the void of your own being, you are bound to be scared, no matter how well you've prepared. Nietzsche was assigned the job of living this horror out for us all. "I love you, I love you" were the words Libby Camp uttered the most in her last weeks.

If a person arrives in a form where there is no first cause for it but only the effect itself, then it is that person's adaptation to her body's annihilation that gives her courage. I think the creatures who are less adapted to their own extinction are the ones who are most full of soul and beautiful. Fear is their loveliest feature. Yes, I am sure that it was weakness, not fitness, that won the physical race to survive in this world. "You sound like an atheist," Tom said. I told him there was an atheist idea in me, alive and well, but you can't really be any kind of "ist" unless you are living out the terms of this idea in your daily life. Marxist, Thomist, feminist, existentialist, Christian or physicist… those are generally just thoughts parading as effective gestures. Libby like Julian the Hospitaller had spent many dissolute years acting out the lamentable influences of her childhood. She drank till she was blind. Got into weed, cocaine, heroin. After she gave much of her money to her dealer, she became a healer. Then she worked towards a degree in alternative medicine. The dainty dab of oil (rose, jasmine, honeysuckle) and her flare with clothes – deep colors in soft textiles, elfin pants and shoes, and only a ring on one thin finger and two little studs in her ears – drew people to her. Squeamish by nature, she learned to wash the shit off the butts of the elderly and give shots to AIDs patients, to massage the ugly and to stick acupuncture needles into the faces of the beautiful. Aquinas said that a person reflecting on certain choices is never closer to acting on a choice than he was before reflecting on them. Libby and I both knew that we had rarely made a choice in our lives; this may account for the forced lack of style in my prose, the absence of personality that I aspire to. I believe that Aquinas also implied that mental reflection is the ability to see what is not out there in relation to what is not in here. Nescience. No one is there.

Libby was a potentially plain and potentially goodlooking person whose face and figure were mesmerizing because of the quick shifts in interpretation the observer was forced to make. Was she or was she not as pretty as she seemed to believe she was? She wasn't plain or pretty. She was plain and pretty. But why did it worry the observer? Her strong jaw, small straight teeth, smooth upper lip, hook nose, bright black eyes, short brow and small ears, the laugh-lines around her eyes and cheeks, could have added up to a classic witch's face. But they didn't. Instead, a volatility in her face made her an original.

3-3

In the hall outside the apartment at 6 pm every evening there is a strong smell of cooking coming from one door – chicken, potatoes, never anything sweet, yet the smell is childish and comforting. Once I saw the elderly couple who live there entering with Christmas packages and they smiled kindly at me. They were exactly what I had hoped would live behind that door because they loved each other when they cooked for each other. If I eat anything, it is small and requires no chopping or grating. An oatmeal cookie and a cup of tea. Cheese on a thumb and a glass of wine. The occasional frozen dinner half-heated. I eat while I work and gaze to my left onto the river and the lights on it. I sometimes watch the news on television and a video I can rent in Central Square. Sometimes I see a show about Nature that treats animals like myths in the making; the program-mers are getting us ready for this metamorphosis. The bumping in the closet is rhythmic at times, almost sexual, except for the humming that goes with it.

I listen from my bed while everything outside the bed grows cold. My children and I used to practically live in bed. We read and ate there on trays. Now I write in bed alone and read in bed but it is not my own writing but the writings by others that keep me from going insane.

3-4

Libby To Me:
Dear Henpecker:

When Oy found out that Oy had this thing, Oy vey! Oy was scared because it meant horse-piddles (hospitals). Our idea of hell? The woyst. And Oy wanted to go to altoynative medicine men asap. But the dox wouldn't let me. Said they were quax. Fux. Don't think I'm just trying to blame (bleem) boys again for everything bad, but Oy am still scared of them! (Remember when they whipped our legs?) Especially the official ones! I hate them. When are you coming (doyty woyd)? Hurry. Ach du lieber, Libby

Dear Heady Hopper:

You wouldnaw believe how bepressed I am to be so beset that everyone thinks I be de-dying. The nice woman dr is the only one who gives me hope (ie continues to torture me). Where are you and why. You should know what sic people like. Someone they love sittin in a chair nearby, not sayin much. A gentle touch on the ravaged brow. Kind woyds. Some music but not too much. Gregorian or Gordian. Flowers, flowahs. They make me feel better. I never

realized why they gave them to sick people. Now I do and
will use them in my practice as soon as I am up and
running. Except I am such a reck, rocked, racked, ruined,
complete and total. (White flowers especially, roses and
tulips.)
Love, Libby

Dear Hen:

I did everything wrong in my life. Face it. I do. I screwed
everything up. There are laws. Why didn't I obey them?
There is such a thing as wisdom. I now realize, and it's too
late. I screwed up out of pride. Now my children are lost
and I have no one to take care of them, and I am alone. How
did I screw up so badly? Why didn't my parents read the
Bible to me? Moses was right! So was Jesus! Mohammed!
Buddha! There are only three big things that count. Living
with God, not judging other people and leaving something
good behind. I didn't do any of those things. And now I'm
scared. And when they said don't divorce or sleep around
or steal or kill or commit adultery with a friend's husband,
they were right too. I'm scared shitless. Literally, I can't shit.
Dots come out. They're agony like torpedoes but dots. I
fucked up. They're like burning coals. Royally. But I want
another chance, God, help, come back. You've been gone six
hours already. I'm in pain.

Dear H, I love you I love you I love you
Dearest Darlingest Best First and Last—

People dont believe it when someone is dying no matter
how much they want to. They dont believe it any more than
they really believe in God. I can see it so clearly because it's
me not believing too. People come to see me and try to
cheer me up, it's hoddible, they cant, because they hate
themselves so much. People hate themselves. So then I make
the pigeon face and the brisk walk nostril face and they
laugh. I think maybe Jesus really believed that little girl was
dying, and so he said Get up, Girl, and she did. If someone
would just believe I was dying, and tell me what to do about
it, the way he did, with practicality and love, I would get
up and walk like that cripple in the cartoon who threw
down his crutches when he saw the walk sign in traffic.
Maybe if they just put signs around instead of coming to see
me. Like "Jesus is coming instead today." Help. Sometimes
I hate them all visiting and am BORED. I have to make
conversation while they test their nerves by staring at the
tubes coming out of my chest and butt. Pathetic. And now
you're in the hospital too and cant come to see me. I hope
you die on the same day I do and we can be buried together
in Mount Auburn Cemetary under the willow tree. No, I
dont. Live, live. Did you get the white flowers I sent you?

3-5

Libby who once loved reading Gandhi lay stark naked on
her bed except for an orange half-slip in an apartment we

shared. The doors were open and so were her eyes. She never knew how she got home that night. She was ashamed later and so I didn't tell her.

Kept silent from her that she had been dropped on the floor inside our door, had crawled stripping to her bed and when I looked out to see who had done that, it was her father the curator climbing into a waiting cab. Maybe she remembered and didn't want to tell me what had happened and she pretended she had blacked out and I pretended I had been sleeping when she got home. I lived out the rest of our friendship not knowing what she knew about that night. Her uncertainty about herself in the world was legitimized by my silence so I will be judged not by history but by God for that.

If you still desire a thing, its time has not yet come. And when you have what you desired, you will have no more desire, instead you will have time. Weak desires protect you from disappointment. But nothing keeps you safer than being a visible ruin.

3-6

Midwinter in New England makes me recoil, especially on those nights between Christmas and Epiphany when darkness is extended like a snake's shadow. In the building there is hardly any activity, except down in the boiler room where the superintendent spends his time. He is lean white and around forty with a welcoming but anxious expression or if pride in his job and irritation at the existence of the people he is working for are engaged in parallel play.

He eagerly offered to fix things which he never fixed. He knew I came from people like his, because he was cousinly with me. When I left the building by turning left off the elevator and heading to the back streets, he was always in that little room with the radio on. The tenants were still away for Christmas and New Years, and only a few grandchildren came and went, using their grandparents' apartment for wild unsupervised parties. Grandparents often suffer from a morbid preoccupation with the safety of their grandchildren, then spoil them dangerously.

One day just before New Years there was an electrical shortage in the building and the superintendent had to take a flashlight and lead people in and out of their apartments. I arrived while he was busy with someone else, saw the elevator was out of order, and mounted the ever-darkening stairs to my floor. When I got there I had to take two turns which made the little light behind me weak then useless in the blackness that stretched ahead and over me. I wanted to persist, went forward wondering if this was what perishing felt like. The blackness became infused with its own form of gravity. I turned back. If all us people only had to adjust to a blackness like that, I suppose we would. Blindness for blind people is actually grayness. I held the wall until I saw the pale light at the top of the stairs. Having lived on the periphery of several wars and urban riots and having been the focus of personal violence, I feel that a devil is always

just around the bend even while I am speeding up images
of Jerusalem.

3-7

"Everyone has one idea of freedom that allows no one else
to have another." When Libby sat across from me, her
children rolling their heads to and fro on each knee, she was
advocating a religious group with a guru whom she adored.

I could tell she had already smoked weed today because her
rational faculties were not good. She couldn't even make a
face or a joke. She droned and this was so unlike her, I
believed she had fled her own body and been replaced by
an alien. My kitchen was a mess. Neighborhood children
were all over the house. My musical husband had gone to
New Orleans. She needed shelter while she and her kids
looked for a place to live.

My house was teeming with people. Two Africans, a West
Indian and a white woman who smiled as if she had wind.
And countless children. The house was built alongside
Franklin Park at the end of the 19th century, purchased for
twelve thousand dollars during the Deconstruction period
when lots of us were renovating old wrecks.

We learned how to caulk, nail, paint, sand, shine with
polyurethane, how to balance at the top of a ladder and
clean up after ourselves. Libby was still carefully avoiding
this kind of labor. Somehow she found her way into ready-

made living quarters with thick buffered carpets and shining bathrooms. While I grew sloppy and thick, she remained streamlined perfumed and light-fingered in her gestures. She made her living spaces into colorful new age lolling spaces with huge bright pillows flopped here and there and healthy plants in every corner and window. These were the leftover effects of her flying dreams, when she spread her arms and soared atop green mountains. The father of her children wanted to be rich and famous without working. He even tried movie-making and ended up running his father's billion-dollar real estate business. He was handsome and clever. He manipulated Libby and their kids in such a way that they believed they owed him something. Imagine if you were born a dollar bill the life you would have. Imagine if you were the thing that got the other thing, the thing equal only to the thing it got, the thing both held onto and quickly discarded.

Usually a person feels like the one who wants or the one who is wanted. One forgets to notice that one also feels like the thing that gets the thing that others want forgetting that one wanted that thing too.

After her stay with me, Libby's children's father gave them the apartment in New York, plus a new man to take care of them. None of them minded anything. They were all individuals, all free for that time, and imagined their liberty would last into infinity because their religion supported the notion of justification by fate alone. If you were born rich, you deserved it. He went away to make his fortune while she stayed behind with the new man, and was the casual caretaker of their children whom she loved. The new man was a drug dealer. We know our parts well, all of them individually. It is the whole we can't see or how our parts form an integrated contradiction. "The supreme Self is attained through the act of hankering…. This requires praying for its consummation before everything else." She gushed this to me and we both cracked up over the word hankering, laughing ourselves across the floors onto stacked pillows.

Libby was like a woman who wears skirts and no underpants because she lived in a state of protest that nobody noticed. She would on the one hand steal a little, lie a little, and then she would also sneak away to meditate, her heart hankering.

3-8

Lewis on the sunbeam in late afternoon at age twenty was smiling widely. He was dressed in jeans, a tee-shirt, and a jeans jacket with some hippy embroidery sewed into the back. That sewing was another thing women did for their boyfriends then. I pretended to be a nice girl and learned how to sew too, in case it would make him love me later. ("There is," according to Lukacs, "no longer any spontaneous totality of being.") "What is that thing on your back?" I asked with a fake smile.

"A mandala but I know it looks like a flat tire."

"But you like to wear it. Why?"

"I have to wear it, or else."

"She would have a fit, if you didn't?"

"Almost. Almost."

"Is she here? Are you going to marry her?"

"In the kitchen," Lewis said stretched and stood and pulled me by the hand like a sister. "There she is," he said pointing at a small wiry-haired girl with huge clothes and glasses and the giveaway slanting shoulder from carrying a bookbag to classes. In that arm she now held a motorcycle helmet. It was, I would later discover, his. He had ridden his bike east from his hometown in Missouri.

This girl would be the first in dozens I met over the years, all of them pointed out to me by a questioning Lewis. "Is she good enough? Am I?" She was a type that repeated though there were two other types too. All of them had skinniness in common, expensive shoes and dark hair. (Weight and shoes are the two giveaway signs for money.) But some were black, some Latino, some Jewish, a couple were Irish, and one was Libby. Lewis never married. He grew decisive, influential, wealthy, instead marrying his work and remaining faithful to it. Girlfriends always stayed in touch long after they broke up with him.

The first time we met, Lewis drew me out the back door of the kitchen into the garden and asked me what I thought of his girl. Not much, I said sternly. Given the fact that I was a narrow stick, it was a pathetic response. The buds were pulsing in me from the cool wooden branches that spurted pink. A spray of forsythia gilded the picket fence at the end of the lawn and crocuses broke melting ice clusters dimpled and dirty. The grass crackled and squished. "Where are you from?" I asked.

"Post-Bellum, Missouri."

"What? Po what?"

"No, no. Missouri. Not misery," he said. "Sort of. Everywhere is beautiful in spring. Everywhere."

And he began jumping as high as he could to bat at a dogwood branch that was dangling as if under weighty ice. He jumped and jumped while I watched like a fan. "My family came up there after the Civil War," he said, "and settled on a small farm." He had a gravelly voice with hard R's from living out there.

"How many?"

"Well, now I have my parents, an aunt and my brother. They're still there."

"Do they miss you?"

"Of course, but my father has his work."

"What kind?"

"Intellectual. We're middle class, in case you're wondering. Not poor. Do you live here?"

"I live nearby, in an apartment."

"Going to Radcliffe like your friend Libby?"

"No, I'm not going to any college. All I want to do is go to the movies."

"Seriously?"

"Until I can make them myself. I love movies."

"Well, you better start learning now. Soon, before you get too old to learn anything new, the way people do."

"I wonder how to begin."

"I know someone who might be good," he said and called back on his way inside. "I'll introduce you. I'll help you. I'll help you." I didn't follow in case he might guess that I was going to dog him for the rest of my life.

3-13

The Lewis-and-Libby love affair was a secret from me while it was happening but I received a full account soon after and realized that I was making a study of the anatomy of a cemetery while they were making out. Mount Auburn Cemetery was founded in 1831, the first in the Rural Cemetery Movement in America. Here the idea of a flowery and manicured graveyard (a garden) led to the reinvention of American parks. The act of creating little Edens in the midst of industry and commerce was in fact an act of lyrical resistance. As with all long-lasting resistance movements, it began in love. In this case, love of flowers. It was autumn when I was there and all that was left in bloom was Chinese sumac, a few old chrysanthemums and witch hazel. But never did a place look more like a 19th century engraving with dots of descending tints and a distant view of hills and a city. The landscape consists of a series of hillocks and ponds, ups and downs, showering shrubbery and clean-cut grass. In October I was studying the Northwest corner, from the Asa Gray Garden down Spruce Street to Crocus, Vesper, Western, and Mayflower Path. Bigelow Chapel including the crematorium was very busy all year. I remember that day there was a large party of bereaved African Americans outside, milling around the statue of the Sphinx – a statue built to commemorate the preservation of the Union after the Civil War and the destruction of African slavery. Everyone there, I could see, was unaware of the existence of this statue and stood around examining it in astonishment.

Meanwhile in New York Libby and Lewis were strolling around Central Park, near the museum, not yet touching but bumping against each other excitedly. Fewer leaves had fallen there. The day was gold and warm and crowds speeded around them on a variety of wheels and even horses. Jogging had not yet been discovered by the public. The Cold War was over. All four assassinations had recently been accomplished and the country was, unknown to its citizens, moving towards a rightwing takeover, which would climax in a violation of the Constitution, bombings of other countries, and the establishment of military alliances with dictators.

For me that day – marble, bronze, slate and Roxbury puddingstone – sculptures that epitomized the late Romantic idealism that we associate with nationalism and a sentimental view of Christianity – and for Libby and Lewis – pulsing glands, quickened heartbeat, heat in groin and palm, the ache to reach each other's breath and find the taste of existence, etcetera.

The city's business banged on around them and from what I was told, they tried to ignore the magnetic pull between their bodies. They tried because of me. My presence between them was an embarrassment. It must have been like the Triumph of Chastity where veils are whirled from the two hands of an innocent woman through shadows warding off lust. Or as if Lewis and I had had years of humiliatingly great sex together, sex that had brought each other as low and as high as you can go and the spirit of these contacts hung over the two of them. In any case there was a brief resistance and then they rushed back to Libby's place. Later she reported that he was "not that good" and offered to describe it all to me in detail but I said no. They had several more encounters in upcoming weeks trying to justify the first one until finally they stopped, blaming their sexual failure on the ghost of my interest looming up between them. But I knew that they simply lacked the lapping fire that one cannot arouse for just anyone.

I was writing my essay on the cemetery and having a romantic friendship with a much-older man. He was famous and so was his wife. I was his secret though not his lover and Libby told me about her affair with Lewis only when she believed that I was safely involved otherwise. She always confused fame with security. "You won't mind if I slept with Lewis?"
"No. You deserve him. You were there first."

A pittance is a meal that a monk eats. I lost my appetite and a decision was made. I would give away everything I loved after that.

SEWING WINGS FOR SWANS

4.1

Tom is reading theology in the bathroom at the border place we call the hermitage, the compound, the pile of sticks, the ashram, etc. Palm leaves like overturned baskets hide us from the daylight. The fire is up, the rain is guttering down the windows, there is a crackerish smell of binding and old carpeting. I am tidying up happy to be a servant to objects. Outside there is the garden sunk in California's winter rains. We are not far from the border where helicopters buzz over the canyons snooping out aliens. Sometimes the officers think they see UFO's after midnight when they look up from their spotlights in the canyons. Tom knows about life in the canyons around us – from Gemma, the prisoner he visits at the jail lounge where we first met – Gemma with the beautiful son – and we often bring food and clothing to those hiding out close to the border.

Today there is no buzzing or hunting, so the rain brings emotional relief. Each part of the compound is raised on stilts to avoid succumbing to mudslides. It consists of five small houses and one larger communal house, and one toilet, all connected by wooden hallways raised up from the sand.

"Where were you during the riots in Attica?" Tom asks me over flushing water.

"Not far from here actually."

"Were you aware politically?"

"Yes, I'd say I was."

"So what did the riots mean to you?"

"Criminals are potential revolutionaries."

"Were you upset to learn this?" he asks stupidly.

"I was happy."

"You must have been really young."

"Around twenty. When George Jackson was murdered."

"Why weren't you in college?"

"I didn't get into any. I was a bad student. I acted up. Joked around. They wouldn't recommend me to anywhere and all my friends went to good places."

"I was twenty two when Bobby was shot," he tells me.

"Where?"

"Boston, of course. All those murders drove me to law school."

Tom continues reading then while I continue dusting the bookshelves. His curls are dust-colored, tight, grayish and his large brown eyes are marked by thick almost demonically pointing eyebrows. He has a soft sensual mouth that stiffens when he reads, and his face is swarthy in complexion. He is quite hairy. He hates his body and his looks though he is very handsome to me.

Now he reads to me from Novalis with a question in his voice: "Destiny and the soul are twin names for a single concept. Do you think that's true?"

"No," I say, "although both are equally blind."

What is between us is nothing. There is nothing between us. Nothing is love, because if you add anything to zero, it becomes a word. The air is thin for us but it is as if we each had two little darts lodged in our flesh in exactly the same spot and they moved in relation to each other like charged needles that seek a thread.

Gold is not here to be used as a color because it is in every color already. In fact Florensky wrote, "Gold is pointless... It is not a color but a tone." I think everything is always an open secret the way the gold on objects is constant and unremarked. Light manifests what is alive in the dark. Some people in the world believe that they can manifest new forms out of their imagination; but there are no new forms where all the materials are the same.

Meditate on the difference between the Important and the Essential, I have heard, and you will learn something secret.

A form cannot be recognized unless its image already exists in the body that discovers it – is an idea as old as bodies themselves.

The musician Messaien said, "It's extraordinary to think that the Hindus were the first to point out and use, rhythmically and musically, this principle of nonretrogradation that is so frequently encountered around us.... We carry these rhythms in ourselves: our face with its two symmetrical eyes, two symmetrical ears, and nose in the middle; our opposite hands with their opposed thumbs; our two arms, and the thorax in the middle; the tree of our nervous system with all its symmetrical branchings. These are nonretrogradable rhythms." Other musicians like birds break off from the goal-oriented sounds of traditional music, and eliminate the usual structures, creating a sound pattern made out of parameters and crossings, rather than predictable sequences.

4-2

Some people use the word affliction when they mean infliction. They think that making other people suffer is painful to them because someone else made them suffer first. Libby never blamed her life on her father interfering with her but she wished she was not the drunk that her mother was. She experienced her addictions not as afflictions but as weeds that grow in certain gardens wild. No matter how you tugged and pulled, you couldn't ever get them all out of the ground. We wandered the streets together looking for Lewis to feed my passion with glances and surmising. Sometimes we found him and he talked to us. He was debonair even when he was selling encyclopedias door to door. Spring enveloped those last weeks of high school making studies impossible. Our desires were not yet as sexual as they were emotional, like reverse orgasms or what we called Melancholia which was really a pre-coital whine.

Libby necked with a variety of boys but didn't love anyone the way I did Lewis until the romance was over. She, like Lewis, always believed that someone better than the person she had would come along.

"Why should you want to be a single individual once you have realized that you are everything already?" wondered the Hindu mystic Sankara.

4-3

A tree with pretty rubbery leaves is planted outside the kitchen that Tom calls the refectory. The rain is pulling at its thick roots. The rain is almost without air. Solid water flooding ground that is usually as smooth as a plastic cover. Now erosion produces layers of miniscule particles of earth, claylike that mush apart in the contact with water. He is playing Hildegaard's Canticles, the women sing over the rain.

"Hey, do we have anything to eat? We won't be able to get into town," he worries.
"I'll look but I think I can do something with some rice that's there."
Now he will ask if I need help and I will say no I'm fine. We are like birds with our words; they come out as calls rather than conversation.

The kitchen we painted is a plywood box on cement blocks. Here is a big wooden table, there some shelves and chairs. A fridge, stove, sink, and crockery that looks rustic but is store-bought, in other words cheap. The windowpanes seem to be melting against the rain. I watch him hurry back to the library in his slicker — a slippery gray figure like a dolphin, and the silence without him in it is whitish. I find rice, canned tomatoes, spices, limp greens that will wash awake, red wine, green cheese. The light outside seems to dilate and contract, the way I imagine the whole cosmos does, the way the lights in movies do before they go dark. I keep thinking the night part is weakening to let more light through but no. The rain will not stop before the night. We eat in silence after he says a perfunctory grace which changes the nature of eating anyway. I feel grateful for the food and the hour. I keep my eyes on the rushing water on the windowpanes, his eyes are facing his plate, one hairy hand up to his temple where a vein pulses like the throat of a small bird. I wonder why I got old before I was able to love a stranger and if I would have the courage to convert before I died. Then I wonder if he has had enough to eat and tell him there is more. He gets more and begins to talk now in a rush the way people on airplanes burst out of silence with the arrival of their plastic trays. There is nothing I think sadder than the clink of forks and knives on cheap crockery coming from unseen people eating.

We have often had this particular exchange about climate and landscape and why we both feel so lonely here uprooted. It was what each of us had wanted of course.

Besides wanting to experience a place we hated, we wanted to be insomniacs and loners, losers and drop-outs. To know the sky was the only location of meaning and joy left to us. Also I wanted to decide if I should assume the care of the blind child or not, when what I really desired was a life of seclusion. I was gladdened by the exit out the backside of the brick building onto small snowy streets when it came time for me to be in the present.

4-4

My mother the maid called herself a "Roosevelt man" until Truman dropped the H-bomb. Then it was clear to her that even liberals can do wrong. She was smart but split. She had the pretensions and airs of a 19th century European procurer, pandering to her employers, then despising them as soon as she was out the door. It's already hard enough to love and judge a person simultaneously, without pretending to love and to judge them.

I asked her: "Mother, how do we prove ourselves worthy of love?"

The daylight on whiteness was a mother's slap to me. It jolted my eyes into their sockets, my limbs lurched forward and a snap hit my skin, my cheeks. Little wooden houses huddled away from the brick. Now I was nearly in the commercial zone. A deli came first then an expensive wooden furniture designer. Dread leveled what little happiness had not already drained away after a few paces. This was an automatic response to entering a public space that was also the site of childhood. Soon people would see me. I don't guess why no one else I know seems to carry this burden of embarrassment. My friends have always hidden me away respectfully. They have helped me to live obscurely as if they could, in doing so, preserve a secret reserve in themselves. Lewis told me to do one thing in the world which was good for other people and which had nothing to do with making money or friendship. He admired philanthropists for instance. He wanted me to sacrifice myself and not wait for someone else to do it for me. Lewis was someone who believed that artists know exactly what they are doing while they are doing it and we fought about this. All artists – painters, poets, playwrights, musicians – were discussed by him in terms of an idea they were trying to express, not in terms of a physical problem they were working through. "I think artists are like blind children on a new campus… More than most people, they trust what they don't know," I told him in the dark of the car and got no answer.

A white sofa, shined wooden floor, a white counter top, wooden stools, a white table shoved against the wall beside a window looking out to the river. When the sun is high and wavy these brick wings can be gloomy. The shade between them is like a hat's shadow creating a sense of selfhood and mystery. When I look out around two I feel like a child who has to go to school and hates it. Every gesture is directed at the air: "Please bring me happiness!"

4-5

In this dream Libby was like someone who had been stretched on a rack, her bones broken and folded. Thin and brown and dressed in orange, she was still making her way around on her own. A chimpanzee was doing the same, long-armed and easy, he entered and departed the small

SEWING WINGS FOR SWANS

ancient spaces of this dream. A mailman wouldn't give me
the large envelope addressed to both of us, green and
winking its joke: "You've Won A Million Dollars" until I
was near tears from wanting that money. It looked as if she
had left me something. Some mark, after all, of our being
best friends. A joint bank account in the afterlife. If this was
India, they didn't say so but I felt Home at last!

When we were children we wanted to swing through trees
so we went on our way home from school to the cemetery
down near the plot where Mary Baker Eddy was buried. We
took turns hurling ourselves forward on a willow branch,
hanging on tight and over a tepid froggy pond where the
waters of the dead flowed up from under.

And now a chimp sat with us even on my lap eating
stonewheat crackers but saying nothing. I wanted to ask him
if he had been the cause of AIDs. They all said it began with
monkeys in Africa. But they always exoticized diseases. The
chimp was as wiggly as a toddler and Libby was sorting out
her clothes with her last energies. She had lots of clothes.
Salted porridge with brown sugar or maple syrup, and a cup
of tea with cream and honey in it. Buddha gurgling or was
it the fountain and the impatiens adding color but no life
to the flower beds. On film the snow came down in wet
cottony lumps and stuck. It was about the night we three
walked up a hill outside my house, and the stars fell around
us in a cone, and although Lewis was invisible, he was the
only one we could really see. And he in turn saw into the
future. He called out – remember, God? – "We thought we

were invisible, but ah, oh no, they will find us out!"

4-6

I had begun to structure myself piece by piece in my father's form. To stay close to his image, to keep myself sane by emulating him. I pretended I was him – a man of poetry, war and honor. I was only five when he died and I had photos on top of the early memories. He had sent me seven little notes about the trees and birds in Korea, about beauty and revolution. He seemed to know he would die and wanted to teach me something of his mind. Sometimes it occurred to me that he might have gone AWOL, and not died at all, because he wanted to be rid of my mother who was a job. All jobs are tests and he brooded over me, year to year, like an angel with an inkless pen.

Lewis like my mother was a lapsed Catholic. She said proudly that she had even refused to baptize me. Lewis had left his interest in law behind as soon as he had a degree in it. He was now, like my father, a journalist committed to undermining almost all governments and famous people.

The sun begins in the night and ends in the middle of my head. It sets down my spine. As for the moon it always seems to float unscientifically wherever it wishes like a paper plate on water, upside down is so flat and light it drifts without law. When the Anchorites in the first centuries after Christ went to the desert, they went looking for a father who had become pneumetaphoros. When they found him they all lived together. In such a community a person could study human behavior, contemplate God and learn scholarly matters in a peaceful and fruitful environment. Community, rule and abbot were and remain the three consistent features of such a life. The rules are: obedience, conversion of life and stability.

I told Lewis about Tom and he showed a brief interest in ashrams and skeets and spent a half hour lecturing me on the moral dimensions of a life spent in retreat. Mad or bad, busy or lazy. He in his wheelchair and me on the edge of my seat, pressed across my elbows on the table on alert for any sign from him – that he might after all admire me in return. But Lewis was someone who couldn't even utter the word "love" instead emitting subtle signs of affection through his eyes which didn't know what they were shining. Chicken, sushi, beer and saki, hailstones ticking on the cars and tar outside. "Look, if you want to find the meaning of life, all you have to do is read the 4th chapter of *Bambi*, the 12th chapter of the Gita, and go see *La Strada* again.... *Bambi*, The Baghavadgita, *La Strada*." That was it. The mention of a movie set us off, our shared passion, what we had seen, what we wanted to see, what we thought of this actor and the way a thing was filmed. "Take the trees, the way John Ford films them, out in the west..." I was speechless in his presence although I was speaking, always pretending to be a bundle of joy but stuttering the way it was with teachers when they asked me for an answer. Articulation, reserved for my children and rages against my husband, failed face to face with others.

This way he could talk freely about himself and project and interject a few observations about and at me. My silence gave him the liberty to say all he needed to about the difficulties of his life as a tyrant. As if I didn't know it! The gunshot, people said, had taken away his desire along with his mobility. Still he continued to write articles and produce films and do much of his work stark naked in bed with a woman wishing around the edges. These women believed he couldn't have sex at all and they said they didn't mind.

"What a laugh," said Lewis. "When you have phony relationships, you watch the misunderstandings develop and you get bored with them, indifferent and fucking up visually, for the fun of it. Not the fun. Not the fun. The interest. To have some. I can see the girls around me getting incredibly agitated, as if I was a dog on a bed. Each one thinks she is going to be the one to turn me back into a man, or to find out, once and for all, if I am impotent. It brings out the sadist in me. I like to watch them flounder. That girl Irene's friend Susanna I think is her name…"

What his purpose was, in telling me all this — I now understand — was his mother's absolution. He had always had the feeling that I was a stand-in for her, and could praise him back to sanity just because I never did. And his now round face swelled into a grimace intended to be a grin. Lewis had grabbed and held me many times, stuck his hand inside my safety belt and squeezed, jammed me against the car door while standing to fall inside and had held me there breathing into my hair. The night trees flashed past a figure

going forward at the same rate that they moved backwards
Transmigration of souls is about leaving one form of being
behind for another while reincarnation means renewing a
former state. Enforced transmigration follows a spinal
injury, among other kinds, when a person is smashed into
a new form. Or maybe it was still him but more. A bigger
boss than ever, a smarter thinker, and a deeper feeler. He
gave presents to those whose time he had abused. Little
things like boxes and pins. To keep me in his pocket for life,
he paid no attention to me or anything I did. His hand
would idly twirl me around and then drop apart and reenter
the world at large. The laughing boy had become a detached
man. "All that is personal soon rots; it must be packed in
ice or salt," are the words Yeats gave to it.

Before the shot Lewis had been bold, traveling the globe's
trouble-spots as a front-line journalist, hanging from the
masts of oil tankers in the middle east, squatting in tunnels
with terrorists, starving with revolutionary armies in Africa,
being shot at and missed. He had no interest in the west,
only in developing countries, and sometimes as one of the
few black American journalists he was asked to negotiate
with political leaders. America made use of his America-
hatred whenever necessary. To describe him as far-left would
not do the complexity of his thinking justice. Ingenuity,
synthesis, amorality and conscience.

He had a fatal awareness of contingencies.

THE HINDU ORANGE OF THE FRUIT

5 1

The ground is brown but I am seeing it grow green under the heavy rain. There is the smell of Darjeeling. Large-grained brown sugar in a dish, cereal, syrup, candy, a few shriveled tangerines. We can't drive down the muddy road again to get food. The floods might wash us right into a canyon. Mud gluts our shoes when we trudge to the refectory. The snakes must be buttoning up their bellies at the speed of the mud. It is spring and they are babies. We stand together at the same window wondering. Tom has been ignoring the violence of the weather as if by dispelling it from his consciousness, it would depart the world. But now I see why. He is afraid that the unexpected will shake his belief in the power of the spirit. My loneliness breaks out of me like a beak inside a shell – it cracks and fills me while he bites his nails and his throat grows tight. "What's going to happen?" one of my children used to ask again and again when we went out walking. This question is written all over him facing the window.

Ramakrishna said: "I used to perform sadhanas in the Panchavati. A tulsi tree grove grew up there. I used to sit in it and meditate. Sometimes I would become very anxious and cry, Ma! Ma! or I would cry, Rama! Rama! When I used to cry, Rama! Rama! I would wear a tail and sit down in the attitude of Hanuman. I was crazy. At that time, while I performed the worship I would wear silk garments and would experience bliss."

"Why don't you meditate and think about Ramakrishna under the tulsi tree?" I suggest to Tom like a mother. Obediently he sits in the armchair, hands on knees, eyes closed, while I stay at the window watching the moving coat of water on the windowpane. A shimmering jelly. But the sky is lighter now.

One of the secret vocations – to be a monk. I wonder why so many know so little about this calling and so lose the chance of a lifetime. To be an old-fashioned closeted gay would be in so many cases the vital ingredients for this life of retreat, ritual, art and prayer. (Was Tom gay? I didn't dare ask!) Or to be Blake instead for whom self-annihilation without celibacy was the goal. His work was his obscurity. You can actually work in opposition to fame. Between the seer and the seen – a blinding stillness. A light cold white line on salt water is the world's resting-point out.

Recollection is for those incapable of meditation. It is the gathering up of all loose bits of memories and compressing them into an image the size of an eye.

5-2

Seen from inside my camera a young woman sleeping forms a slovenly image. The lights have gone out after an earthquake downstairs. The bed has rolled away from the wall and her dog has returned home, unfed, for cold manicotti, shivering. However it is not my foster daughter but a stranger sleeping there. To wake her is only to feel a terrible rage at this intrusion even after a natural disaster, I push her physically out the door to her car that has been in an accident. I can't bear to watch her drive away, run inside to plug in the electric phone upstairs to see how my twin son is and a woman on the line is wanting me to edit her natural daughter's film for her application to film school. She has been impressed by one review of my work, the only one. Again I am furious saying yes but how difficult this will be and hang up in her face, two of my short-term foster children watching me over their books. The lights are still shining on my script.

Upstairs in my old big house, there was lots of dust on top of useless mementoes including clothes from Nepal, Greece, stones from Patmos and Dublin, religious kitsch from Libby and Tom and the children. Bay shells from Rosarito and South Beaches all undusted all unlooked-at all given to me as the one who never gets to go away. Dust is pure – a snow that doesn't melt.

The strange girl is so slow to wake, sunk so deep into her waiting that it is a numbness. Shaking her doesn't help. She is pretty-lipped but not the Libby I want to see. If she had just had no hair on her head and a wider mouth, glinting eyes and a hook nose, she would have been the person my camera was expecting. Raising other people's children can make all people seem interchangeable as companions and you will take anyone who comes along to fill in the scene, the time. You see a floppy head of hair coming and think It's him! but it's someone who is almost him and for a flash you think I don't mind. I'll go with this one instead. This is detachment. Once I was surprised to realize that all individuals contain the same ingredients: "whoever this is."

Finally the day came, ten years after the promise was made, when Lewis introduced me to the person who would help me work with film. Irene was fat and famous among serious film-watchers, a middle-aged beauty with creamy skin and huge hippy clothes slipping from her soft shoulders. Her fatness was delicious but few wanted to face the fact that heaps of skin can often be divine and seductive, torrents of loose and lickable substance bundling up the bones. I am always a mother but she was always a mother to me. She let me sit in while she edited for several weeks and then I could do it myself, and did. I edited for money and spent twenty years making one film and twenty five dream-videos for love. I want to see. To see so clearly that personality is of no account. Gestures that glide upward – where is their gravity. A child's spit viewed through a child's microscope was my inspiration. It led directly to the smearglass of galaxies and the most perfect sentence of all: "My soul magnifies the Lord."

5-3

Down in the boiler room the superintendent is listening to Senate Hearings and eating a gourmet sandwich from Darwin's Deli. The sandwich – brown bread, avocado, cheese and bean sprouts – is the best he has ever had in his life, and happily he asks if he can help me. I wonder if there is a laundry room in the building. He directs me to the basement, picks his teeth and asks me how long we plan to stay. We have a year's lease, I tell him. Uh huh. How many people? Just two. He makes a lot of noise. Which number are you? 405. Hm. If he asks my last name, he will think I am a Catholic. I am so aware of people hating Catholics as much as Charlotte Bronte did that I want to be one even more. The same people who practice Buddhism and admire Tibetan monks make fun of a Catholic's habits. Many Protestants have become other religions these days and have brought to their practice much of the Puritan mentality of their forebears. They fuss over details and believe that clear accounts will add up to a better life. Antinomian, empirical, intelligent, self-sacrificing and rule-bound. I admire their discipline but I like the way Catholicism is a load of contradictions. Now the rain is letting up and a soft blue light is sifting through the flannely clouds. Gullies of water gurgle down the canyons and birds sing. I feel dread. The opening up of light and sky, the return of the responsibility that the empty air brings, horrifies me. Since God has abandoned the world, it is time who is left watching over us. Time is the spirit who breathes into the world. When it was raining, water was like an apology. The super doesn't ask me anything more.

5-4

The way the arms of the oak bounce reminds me of Siva beckoning and laughing. I think maybe Hinduism will guide us through the dead wood of Christianity and into fresh new greens. I was an existentialist, then I noticed how words could make things happy again. Many of the most lost people used the loveliest language in order to laugh. No hospitals but deranged and homeless movement from house to house, city to city, phone booth to public toilet. No college for them! This was how McCool found me watching him – himself more insane, more poor, more lost than some others. All of these qualities mashed my worries. Rolled them aside like trash. McCool was all feeling and fast-talking. He combined several of the aspects of God that we dread (i.e. Satan's), the ones that allow children to compete, produce wars, massacres, infidelities, that allow sea-elephants to stop evolving and insects to remain machines. We met in a pub at a sing-along. Nobody cared I was there. They thought I was just a 21 year old hat check girl with a needle and thread, and I was. Some beings see the world as a palace. Some see it as a marketplace. Some see the future as a malign region. Others wait for something wonderful to arrive before they die. I always carried a sewing basket to work.

If you think you need to fly into outer space for a surprise, just go and look at some spider monkeys, a hipppotamus, an aquarium where there are fish with eyes in their spines, four mouths and no way in. They are like a secret code that unlocks a public event. My body continues to puke and yearn, withdraw, hesitate and jump out of danger. Is resting the goal of lusting? Virginia Woolf had wanted a steel body to clasp all the fluttery parts of her mind in an embrace. This became her butterfly aesthetic.

I have to keep moving my bones through hardship and ignore the obstacles. It is a kind of machete approach to the day. If I can recollect happiness, and I can, it is usually thanks to artists like God who made nature and Rossellini. Buddhists on the contrary are calm and don't cry for succor (Ravish me, God, please don't leave me alone!) Between a Buddha and a Buddha there is a bowing couple. An economy that proves equality. My kind of prayer is the prayer of a sucker who pleads for one smile from a face that is turned away from her.

McCool always looked me right in the eye accusingly.

Parents usually name a baby before it is born in order to reserve it a space in the angelic tablets. When you pray for a person the man said you must use their name, just as panelists on television must address each other by name so the camera will know where to turn. Wanting only one person to turn in my direction or to call me by my name or to see my films with my name written at the end, I would take a fake name cheerfully and hide the real one.

We married each other in an eccentric livingroom ceremony wanting to be saved by the words that the Unitarian read from Scripture. They were traditional wedding words. McCool wrote music and called me by his name, when we got married, it began with a Q my favorite letter. Question, Quest, Quidam and Queer. It felt good having a Q there. It compressed my fragmented alphabet of a name into one letter. Put a magnet in the center and sucked the others in. Like the child of a drunk, I listened too acutely to the shifts in McCool's enunciation, not looking for a slur, but for an Irishness that would make me quiver with pleasure. His Irish accent came and went in strength. It was like losing signals from my father in outer space. When the accent was weak, I felt less safe. After all, he was infertile, so I was too. I had the foster babies instead – twins in one year, then one more one year after. Ruled them and played with them. "You have attained existence through my body" was never to be my experience. A Buddha can have thousands of eyes but God has arranged things so that eyes are dispersed equally among ordinary creatures.

Children's eyes followed me trustfully everywhere while McCool's were filled with suspicion and hate. "Who left this magazine here?" he might ask threateningly.

"I don't know."

"Yes you do. Who."

"Oh it might have been Father Julio."

"Liar," he laughed.

"He came here for you too."

"I bet. I'll go look for him."

Julio Solito was a parish priest who practiced Yoga and read Hindu scripture. We knew him very briefly, a small man with a starving face—that is, a face that seemed to be fleeing starvation, he rushed through our lives like a coke-head, at full speed.

McCool liked him and considered him a true revolutionary
– that is, someone who lived out his beliefs. Ironically he
was sure that a priest wouldn't sleep with a woman
especially me. He went to find and have a drink with him
but soon he was suspicious of something else.

My husband hated most people including me. Strangely, he
didn't realize this. He thought it was all kinds of other
things that were the problem with me. He was handsome
for one thing, and couldn't understand how he could be
married to one ordinary person. He was gifted, a musician,
and charming, and very smart, and so how could he only
have one person at home to listen to him. I was an awkward
woman so why was he bothering to be jealous of me unless
there was something I was really doing bad to him. Julio
politely said, "He just doesn't appreciate you." This priest
was reticent and miserable, having come from the
Seychelles into our drab slum parish. He had an international perspective, my husband would say. He was shocked
that poor people in America said they were poor, himself
having been in Tanzania and Bangladesh. When he left he
didn't even say goodbye, only one more sign of his detachment. I felt a mission in him that was inspired by interfaith.
He was one of the old school of heroic tormented priests
who live in poor communities; who are tolerant, ironic and
solitary.

He might have said: "Beings are numberless, I vow to save
them. Desires are inexhaustible, I vow to end them."

Years later – when we were friends – I told Tom about Julio Solito as if trying to shame him by the example of this perfect priest.

He cried out: "Julio Solito? But he was the father of Gemma's child." We both fell against the wall simultaneously.

Buddhism says, "In all things there is neither male nor female." And Jesus too said sex was meaningless in the kingdom of heaven. You can build around a space, but not build the space itself. A black hole is a spiral that rotates and drags stuff into it, it may be the home of ghosts, the goblet that drinks the drinker or the cone where God changes its mind and pulls everything back in again. If the universe is swelling and contracting, it sounds like a woman to me.

Gray winter branches scratch glass till it sings. My husband meantime played guitar and penny whistle and sang traditional songs. He had once been close to the Clancy Brothers and their friends in New York. Blue eyed and black haired, he spoke in rushes of free association linking local politics with Dante, a city sewage system with Pilgrim's Progress, and Weil with Virgil. He had managed to create a new identity for himself and a new passport and with the US Savings bonds I inherited from my father at age twenty one, we bought our cheap house.

He got along well with everyone who had a particular political take on the international situation; he was paranoid and idealistic at the same time which is a difficulty. There was lots of sitting around yelling. News items cited and columns and men. Theirs was a closed masculine system which grasped contradiction but never found a way to transform it into paradox because that would have been too complete a solution. To solve a world problem was frightening to them, for resolution had something of death in it, the death of their own perplexity and excuses. He said he was orphaned in County Carlow and raised by brutal and intelligent Brothers of the Holy Cross. He was distraught at his own infertility and often insisted it was my fault, and swore if he was just with someone else…. He wanted the children raised Catholic in order that they establish an identity with him, even though he called himself lapsed. He wanted to make tons of money fast, yet he had contempt for the new rich. Instead he appreciated the sagacity of the longtime wealthy. He was verbally violent towards most corrupt politicians except those corrupt politicians who had his interests at heart. If only he had known what his interests were! His confusion was his downfall. It was 1968 and the students were rioting. My husband was no fool but he was a coward. He got things wrong almost every time in order to steer clear of commitments. Yet simultaneously he was almost always right about other people's weaknesses and temptations. He was a great supporter of women's liberation and especially of women having children, taking care of them and working to support everyone all at the same time. He pinched the children's cheeks, gave me my orders for the day and left the house with a bang. My relief at his departure was the key to the paradox: I would do any amount of slave-work in order to be free.

5-5

The superintendent says: "I knew a family with your name in Dorchester. Any relation?"

"I don't know, there are so many."

"The Irish in Boston are pigs," he said. "I'm Italian. They kill you if you go in one of their Shamrock bars and shit. Gotta be Irish to be safe going inside one of them."

"I know."

"I know you know. The ones in Ireland I hear are different."

"You mean the Irish?"

"What happens when they cross the water?"

"They become American." He threw a brown bag in the wastebasket and remarked: "Though I have to say, the Italians stayed pretty much the same low-life fools they always were. With the exception of Martin Scorsese... Imagine if you were black what people would do to you in this city."

I walked along the riverside, cars beating by, and reflections like fish in dresses were sequined on the water top. Dusk, lights, more colors than seemed possible were dotted on the screen, de-iced since sun had returned. I strolled over the walkbridge to the other side of the water and paralleled my path back northwest. The brick building did not reflect, but held its shape into itself. Some crows' raw cries split the air inside the trees. Not far ahead was the cemetery settling down for the night. An oblate is buried in a cowl but my mother was cremated in a cardboard box. Sometimes I thought I heard her banging to get out, but it was probably the Bumper (as Julio dubbed him) inside the apartment with me.

5-6

I can't explain myself, God. It is as if my camera, my film and even a screen are reeling me in to my story and no one is operating them. A horse gallops down an oncoming road that is severed by a river. Oncoming into my head, that is. The road is white and bony like the streets in Antonioni's *The Passenger*. No leaves blow in the holy land but the horse's hooves turn up sheets of dust and a thick nearly creamy substance like the arms and bosom of my film teacher, Irene. I decide to stay paralyzed and accept the arrival of the horse's rider who will seize me without love. I forgot: Never any erotic love as long as I seek God. But it pounds past and I am dusted into a soft substance aghast at nearly dying when the body is everything and everything is a body.

Lewis helped me make my big film that I called *The Mansion of Fun* based on some writings by Ramakrishna. It was an orange film that used a variety of devices for voice-over to quote his teachings. Our actor had once acted as a child for Sarajayit Ray but was now an aging man. He sat at a table in a circle of small orange bonfires, flowers, fruit and smoke, reading into a series of voice machines, then playing them back. He was a very disciplined man, but he believed that the text was written for him. About two thirds of the way through the film, he danced off the set and wasn't seen again. Luckily Lewis with his camcorder captured the whole affair backstage and followed the man weaving off down the snowy streets. We couldn't have had a more appropriate conclusion to the bewildering messages of the film. Ramakrishna was a saint who liked to dress up as a woman or pretend to be Hanuman the monkey. He laughed at his own jokes and experienced raptures that others witnessed. Boys loved him.

They say when you wake up to Brahman, you wake up with the revelation that you are already blessed and the way you know this is that you don't need a witness to know it.

The film gave me more time alone with Lewis than I had ever had or ever would again.

"That which cannot be seen by the eye, that is the Self indeed. This Self is not someone other than you." Someone invisible is more emotional than someone who can be seen. A camera has its own eyes too that are borrowed from a self who lights its way through the lens, and what it has seen is turned around on the screen, and looks back at the eyes that saw it first, but as if it is looking for its origins.

You can write you are a Catholic and look in the mirror and really it is a Jew who looks back at you. These experiences are hard to manifest in images.

A man named Kosta helped us with the editing of my film. He was critical of every decision I made. He was an unknown filmmaker and his bitterness was a trouble to me.

First he was very good at editing. Second he was interfering in the way that only certain small men can be. Third he asked: "What the hell does this mean?" when Ramakrishna said, "The sacred tulsi tree and the stem of the horse-radish are the same thing!"

On the table among the voice machines was a wind-up monkey. The actor played with it while he read his lines and then listened to them. The monkey clanged a tambourine and marched up and down with his tail twitching. Ramakrishna chuckled up the back of his throat. I focussed my camera on his mouth, his hands, the monkey, while Lewis took the long view of the stage and the orange fires.

From there Lewis used Naugasound while I used Walkman sound and stayed close to the actor. In the end sixty pounds of sound alone were collected along with footage and driven through a blizzard to an editing room. "A filmmaker has to take a quantity of pictures to create a single movement, and still the picture trembles when it appears," wrote Strindberg. We worked on synchronicity for three days and through two late nights. We moved whole sections of the performance around, slashing and rearranging and we even added new sound from a different source altogether (the chatter of monkeys and birds at the zoo) and then drove the reels to a mixing room in the suburbs and saw our film projected full-scale on the wall for the first time. I sat in the mixing room with its twenty three mixers that could have been part of a space station, taking notes while Lewis sat in a dark room next door. I could hear him being critical and so I insisted that we take it all back for one last editing marathon. I was crying. Lewis cheered me on and said he would send it to a festival in Rotterdam. He quoted Tolstoi who in 1921 saw a movie for the first time and remarked, "Now we don't have to invent stories anymore. The cinema can show Russian life as it is, instead of chasing after fabricated subjects."

"You can make more!" Lewis encouraged me. "You can. We can make another."

It is when a movie is full-square on the wall that there is nothing more in life to chase after. There is no future. You have reached bliss.

The film went nowhere afterwards. The guys were too busy and tired to fight for its showing and I was a domestic servant who could not sell her wares in the world. Lewis was always running and Kosta needed to move on to another job.

So either it was the world's fault or mine that it never was shown. Or Kosta was right all along and the subject had no commercial value.

I told Kosta that it was my intention that the actor should be its only audience. The world is a mansion of fun. I eat, drink and roll around having fun. He said, "Don't worry, it's a jewel, they survive in the dark." Kosta, a tough little man with a well-carved face, suddenly seemed to understand me and to feel sorry he had not done so before. But this was because I was now a failure like him, he could actually see and hear me. He organized a small showing for a few friends and his Korean-American wife who called the film-space Rotterdam.

TWO SIDES OF A CRIB

6.1

The birds are delirious at the ending of the rain. Perfectly straight strings of water gully from the gutters onto the ground and shine. Sun up and yellow. Colors never brighter than after a gush of water. A lyric of chirrups to fatten the buds, February spring on the border. You know that consciousness is fed by all things living, just the way the eye retains the white of an object.

The day the rain stops a boy about twelve years old comes out of the rain and canyon. White tee-shirt, jeans, no sneakers no socks. He is brown with shaved black hair, a frightened face but one as transparent and pretty as that of a young Yogi. Lost, not well. Not wanting to be found or moved along, he is skittish with us. Asthmatic breathing or something, the steam is rising off the warming leaves and Tom leads him into the refectory for some oatmeal, maple syrup, butter, a hot drink. The boy is shaking, unable to eat or not to eat, and nodding and shaking his head jerkily to the remarks we make in Spanish. Then water as clear as from a sacred brook spills from his lips in threads. The veil around Mary is watery and the veil she spins around the world is water too. Babies break the water and spit it out on entering the air. But where does the water of the spirit come from? How did he have pure water running inside of him? For that moment, as I wipe his lips, I am looking forward to a day when there are no more possibilities.

Tom murmurs, "Another child in need of a home." No, no,

not me, I think. I have done enough for the world. "There are desperate and needy children everywhere, and I'm too old."

"He reminds me of Julio," he says.

"So? Just step down into the canyon and you'll see they're everywhere. People and children, who are homeless."

"Do you think he has family down there?"

"Well, let's go see."

6-2

Slipping over the ice, striped like bacon fat along the pavement, I waved goodbye to the superintendent as he bashed garbage pails around, and hurried to the movies. The theater was in a small brick building that also housed an Algerian cafe and bar.

I was going to see *A Touch of Evil* for the fifth time because I only liked things that reminded me of themselves. In the theater, I was almost the only person there. I found my favorite seat – left side aisle ten rows up – and waited for the fade-out of the lights. The old battered seats felt like a pile of rods under me. I knew that I would have to move if someone ate popcorn near me and looked nervously around at the few others plumped back into their chairs. I was safe from eaters.

To me, making a film – that is, editing in a dark room for days – was the only thing better than watching someone else's movie. It was like being a miner who polishes jewels before extracting them from their stony base. There is no enormity in this process. Erasure of self is its goal. Give me a little screen and a lot of reels or even digital action carried in, and I will say, with Bambi's mother, "Oh, how kind last year's dead leaves are!" What did she mean about the leaves being kind? And she added: "They do their duty so well and are so alert and watchful. Even in midsummer there are a lot of them hidden beneath the undergrowth. And they give warning in advance of every danger."

Do leaves have eyes? Does film?

Henry Adams wrote when he was in Egypt, "One's instinct abhors time." Catholics abhor calendars. Poised and pointed towards an altar instead, they prefer to have feast days with wooden dolls, colored glass, candles, goblets and a gold plate like Akhmaton's disk swept and dusted of the divine in front of their eyes. A different calendar from the rest of us – Advent, Easter, Salvation History and Ordinary Time. Henry Adams was "a Darwinian for fun." He was an atheist but in the spirit of one who wants to protect God from himself. He was disappointed in himself and everyone else. But he remained fascinated by great constructs.

Whittaker Chambers, who translated Bambi from the German with careful poetic attention, was a moralist and a snitch. Some bogs have their own lamps. My husband was fascinated by Chambers, by his genius and his treachery, his secrecy and unacknowledged homosexuality.

His thoughts were tickled with the rage of a hangover after a night of cheap red wine. Hangovers can create entire belief systems along with hot sweats headaches terror. God would always be born in a place of such demoralized flesh. "The existence of evil here below, far from disproving the reality of God is the very thing which reveals him in his truth," wrote Simone Weil. My husband was a true believer when he was having the DTs.

Is it possible that excess bliss is the producer of evil? My husband hated himself, then saw nothing but wickedness and ruin in everything around him, sometimes even the children, calling the twins The Mutants. He didn't like two of them being identical when he had a hangover. Once Libby told him about yoga and he tried to discipline himself without luck. "La Fontaine and other fabulists maintained that the wolf, even in morals, stood higher than man," said Henry Adams, sick with disappointment. But my husband fascinated me, because he was so extreme – too bad and too good for his own good. Goodness should have no force behind it.

6-3

Libby ate in order not to be hungry later while I ate because I was hungry. The difference is obvious. She ate without gluttony, with dainty concentration and pleasure. I gorged and picked with my fingers at leftovers like a ravenous dog who tastes little. She and I broke apart for seven years. She went off with an old friend from our elementary school days, a thin blond girl named Honey Figgls. They headed west together to follow the guru they shared and had what they called experimental sex together. They kept coming back to it. Libby sent me letters from time to time and I always wrote back but her affair with Lewis was a haunt between us. Every metaphor is a description of the world as it is. We raised our children separately and she began her classes in Spiritual Exercises not of the Ignatian kind. They were yoga-based and involved inhaling the colors of the world and saying ah.

There was a mandala in front of her. Under the altar in any Catholic Church is a huge hole that travels to the center of the earth, into hell itself. This altar is the stone rolled across this tomb-like space. To get to the other side of the altar you must fall like Alice down into the hole and spin in hell. There is no hole under a mandala but nonetheless some who have these signs die young. No matter how much you cry I don't want to die! that gravity of the gods is irresistible, and its timing too.

I loved Quincy Bay in the summers where the descendants of starfish, polyps and trilobites rolled in the tides. But the water became polluted before I was a teen and the beaches were only for playing in the sand. Libby came to stay with us – seven years had passed – when she was desperate, her children at her side. We went to Quincy Bay to let them play. She talked non-stop about her religion. She was no longer taking hard drugs and had begun the slow struggle for liberation that almost every addict makes. It was a winter day and one of the children wandered into the sea in her snowsuit. Libby would soon be herself again. I could tell because she was worried about me.

Mornings I went to my job while she had sex with my husband. The twins were in day care in a concrete slab that abutted an old people's home down by the subway tracks. Her children were in a Montessori nursery. She and McCool were alone at home too long and he was a famously good lover, though I never warmed up to him.

She knew this, it freed her as she also worried about my lack of joy, my general poverty. She could see that McCool's and my mutual misery was our only intimacy. We made each other suffer so deeply from our lack of love for the other, we were in hate, a condition that rips two people open until they only know themselves through the eyes of the other. I saw at once he was in love with Libby now and didn't blame him. I wanted her to take him away from me before he murdered me, and she did.

Wolves are faithful and love each other throughout their lives. He and Libby went at it like that. The forest of empty rooms, everyone at work or school, concealed the play of motives between them. Their leaves were my bed. Leaves do have eyes. "The goal of the Unmanifested is hard for the embodied to attain," but sometimes love between two people can get very close to that source. The closer they got, the more they were in a protracted state of sore nerves and yearning for emptiness. I felt sorry for them, and I wanted to be rid of them, the way a mother feels towards sullen teens. My husband begged me, "Don't leave me. Just let me see this through." But I said, "No way! You don't love me. I'm getting out of here" and I bundled up the twins and the little one and laid them out to sleep in the back of our cheap little Opel station wagon and headed west. West is death for mystics and East is the resurrection. About ten miles into my ride, I was elated at what had happened. I was free and he was guilty! I had heard that Lewis was in San Francisco. Henry Vaughan the disagreeable and great Welsh poet wrote: "Though when we travel Westward, though we embrace thornes and swet for thistles, yet the businesse of a Pilgrim is to seek his countrey."

My country was Lewis from whom I was in exile – or was I his devotee seeking a future through him as others seek samadhi? Were we congressional, unselfish, empathetic or out of sync when we were together? I don't remember. Nectar of friendship between Rumi and Shams could have been ours.

Three bowls of ice cream were downed by my children who rolled around in the car, having fun, released from day care and a drafty house. Otherwise we had the ideal food for deportees: a pound of brown bread, hard boiled eggs and salt, oranges, bananas and chocolate.

It was the February spring when we arrived in Oakland and there were fruit trees in bloom, the waxy blossoms flat face up already. Smears and gashes of broken sun across the branches and views of the Bay at sudden turns. Who could not admit that this little portion of the globe shone like that bulb Jerusalem?

Its civic pride good works and resistance to war were epic. Sickle cells under a microscope are watery and various and insects seen up close are enormous, but the suffering of the people here is swallowed by white light. "I am in jail," Lewis wrote back to me, "just for awhile, but please don't forget me. Letters, cuttings, books, whatever. You are precious to me."

He had participated in a sit-in at Livermore and was doing shut-in time with two Catholic priests and a bunch of other protesters. My foster children were my allies. The liberation of children from grown-ups was my plan. All my children could dress themselves for school and this small achievement was part of our strategy.

I went and surprised Lewis behind some bullet-like holes in glass. He was wearing khaki colored prison garb. He was really elated at seeing me and saw me as physical for once. "You look good enough to eat," he said, "to eat, I tell you." I stared at his full lips, the rays of pinkness that lined them inside, and pressed my mouth to the plexiglass. He met mine with his. We laughed, and drew back.

Within a week a crazed McCool – ditched by Libby – arrived out of the northeast and drove us east again. He said, "I don't care what you did, but don't ever let me see you with him."

"Why is seeing so important?" I asked.
"Because I see all these half-breed kids you bring home, and I see some of them look like Lewis and could be his. I see only too clearly. You say you have chosen them, but believe me, I see this word 'chosen' could mean something else."
Soon we were stopping on the edge of California and Arizona at the border canyon compound. McCool announced that Libby wanted me to have it.
"This land is your land," he told me. "Atonement."
"For what?" I asked.

"For our sins, hers and mine, stupid. Libby thinks that we did you wrong. She wants you to have this place. I don't know why. I mean, considering." I saw from the way his face turned to view the property that he loved it. The face of a heart is a face.

I slipped postcards secretly into boxes, addressed to Lewis, all the way home.

6-4

"We have to deal with this child, find his home. I'll go down into the canyons and look," I tell Tom, pulling on my dungaree jacket. "No, we will come too," he says and gently gestures to the child whose face is luminous with fever. He seems to have eyes in all of his cells, there is a diamond fuzz in the moisture covering his cheeks, like the smashing atomic sunshine fuzz that California light is said to have. He follows Tom, lifting his feet up as if they dragged seaweed. The wet is evaporating with supernatural speed. A steaminess coats the trees that still are dimpled with bright bubbles. A rainbow crosses the sky, its colors sharply marked. At night coyotes bay from these canyons and there are fat rattlesnakes lounging on the paths. I have on boots and carry a big stick and sing a song I once loved called "Together Again". Tom follows with one arm loosely reaching back towards the sick boy.

Ninety eight steps up the canyon wall little stones are rough and puddled, a palm paddles the side of a eucalyptus tree. Women have laid out plywood to dry like linen on rocks. Clothing and bedding and trash bags stuffed with food are bundled and rolled neatly into the arms of a wet tree. The women's mouths are ajar like clay pots. They see me coming and murmur to each other, never averting their eyes from mine. It's a scene that reminds me of a neo-realist film made in Italy during the war. I am the camera that makes others self-conscious. There are no men here only four women and one baby and one little girl with straight black hair squatting in over-large sneakers among the women's legs. "Is one of you missing a child?" I ask.
"No, Mama went to Ensenada," I am told.

A really enlightened person only sees colors floating in air where there is an animal in hair with its mouth open. There must be a variety of ugly approaches to the hole yawning under the altar. To be hung, head first, into that pit, would be truly a time to call for help from the outside. I feel that all of us women are in that position, right there, walled by the muddy sludge and the arms of the angel of defecation and poverty.

I remember Libby and other well-to-do people and wonder: Where is the profit in making money when having it is really the point? Libby was born with an income already. Expensive vitamin pills, herb teas, grainy breads and fresh grown fruit. She jumped from pillow to pillow, with a cigarette, an acrobat of jokes trying to make everyone laugh. Sat like a yogi and asked about Lewis. "Does he have a girlfriend? He's so famous!"

She always forgot that I was low-life myself, a penurious and anxious head of household.

Even if I was almost able to report on Lewis, almost had seen him recently, it was almost always me who called him and found him almost happy enough to hear from me to relieve my embarrassment. "He is almost in Jordan now, with his hand-held camera. And he has a girlfriend as always, a woman who throws tantrums, is wildly jealous, has sex with screams, takes a shower before and after, is half English and half Indian, tiny, pretty, intelligent, well-read, classy, and making lots of money as an editor."
"God. I feel like a complete failure."

Libby dying was surrounded by everyone she ever knew. They drifted around her house smoking dope, drinking, laughing, playing music, praying, lighting candles, eating and whispering, carrying her between them and sitting on the side of her bed while she slept. They loved her. The last day they passed a bottle of iced lemony vodka around and around in a circle while she in her white silk pajamas had nightmares induced by morphine and death. She said she was afraid to open a door before she stopped saying anything. I wasn't there but in a hospital half-dead from a ruptured artery. My body wanted to die – had actually planned it that way – on the day that Libby died, but the doctors wouldn't let it. I noticed that the white roses she sent me had frayed yellow hems, but I had no needle. The color cream spreading at its fat part next to the stem was the color of my mother's throat and the ticking along the hems of her dresses.

That day the canyon smells of human shit and a rooster lies clobbered on a rock, its head a red stain shaped like a big beak. One candle burns in a blue glass. Dispassion was the biggest passion ever between McCool and me. One of the women was moving towards the boy, and he was moving in her direction too. It was – when I came out of the movies – dark and white, snow pee-colored under the streetlights and a touch of evil on all cold things. The clouds from the canyon are sand-gold and tumultuous from all the rain. When they lived beside the canyon Libby was overwhelmed by my husband's certainty and let him do whatever extra he wanted with her. My near-monk friend is interested in Tantric sex and actually asks me to purchase a book for him on the subject. Orgasm is not in itself sinful since it exists.

TWO SIDES OF A CRIB

"In the first state there is form, in the second state there is the formless, and, after that, there is the state beyond the form and the formless."

"He look like Jesus," says the woman moving towards the boy. "But not Jesus, my friend's boy. He's this Juan. Maybe. His mother down there."

"He's sick," I tell her and make a throw-up gesture and face.

"Well, bring him to mother. I bring," she says.

We all slide down ninety eight steps through the basin of the canyon littered with lots of paper and cans and up the slippery but not so sheer a slope on the other side. They are silent, even the children, and we all fall on our knees a few times. We are all wearing jeans and sneakers and arrive filthy at another encampment. "Shouldn't we call a doctor?" Tom calls out to me. "Are you crazy? The INS, you know.... They'd all be hauled away."

The soil has begun to resemble a clay and cucumber face wash that Libby used to give me. I tip down towards it.

"He should be examined," Tom insists and, next to last in line, turns back.

"He should be with his mother. Trust me."

"But what if he dies?"

"It's just the flu, or food poisoning. Let's go."

"But where is he?" Tom calls.

All of us turn together. The boy is gone. A stream of water slides off a palm branch onto the ground. The smell of eucalyptus is as acidic as tomatoes and sage, the light-color blue. Birds twirt and rattle. The rest is all green and still.

The Supreme Contemplated ones were of the female gender according to Ibn Arabi who had an angel cosmology, where women appeared and disappeared as manifestations of divine wisdom. Mary herself floats over the world, a see-through figure begging for peace but leaving no trace or effect on what men do. Mary holds her baby through all time crying, "You can't kill him, because he has been made out of nothing!"

God, we looked for the boy for an hour, remember, and returned, speechless, home. He was gone as swiftly as he had come. None of the people could explain, but the women didn't seem surprised or alarmed. "It goes!" one cried, lifting her hands to a laugh.

6-5

Libby when ill loved being cradled warmly in the arms of her friends who were grateful to her for letting them behave well at last. Her bones were palpable, her skin dotted with lesions that sometimes seeped out drops of blood spontaneously. She wore a shunt in the dent in her skull. She also had worn one for drippings in her chest. Once a male nurse punctured her lung looking for a place to dig in the needle. All this time she did not want to die or escape her torturers. She had the discipline that Krishna recommends in the Gita. Morphine and love to burn. Her features turned Tibetan as well as Native American, her face swimming through multiple migrations of meaning. Her sex dried up and disappeared. She kept wearing orange against her cinnamon skin and its lights played tricks.

What if! she cried. Wrinkles cover an elephant's hide, piggy creatures have wet upturned snouts and walk like penguins, there are even terrified bugs and rabbits who have survived.

Her children hung at her bedside like two sides of a crib.

There are mutations following nuclear explosions and germ warfare and birds with oil glued to their wings and beaks. Libby turned into a saint before she died. She might have chanted: "When I say I am God, God, I don't mean that I AM God. I mean that I am God."

Gobblers are turkeys that people gobble up. Evolution from lower to higher, the aggregation of the atom in the mass, the concentration of variety inside of unity and the way chaos is embedded in order – (there were anarchists who were Catholics and Marxists who were anarchists) – these were the concepts that governed generations from the mid nineteenth to the end of the twentieth century.

My husband bragged that he had been one of the men behind the wire in Ireland, after getting caught during some minor IRA scrimmage and released after a couple of years. Now he said he was American thanks to marrying me. But he renewed his Irish passport dutifully. My husband didn't care for me but for his foster children he ususally did. We stayed married although we could have divorced at once. Ireland, too, chose to remain neutral during the war, when it could have supported Britain during World War Two, made a deal ending partition and this way have avoided fifty more years of slaughter.

6-6

To Ibn Arabi the human creature is both pre-eternal and post-eternal and manifests itself in its earthly body (the middle) in multiple and simultaneous forms. There are no sequences but vibrant occurrences and conditions all over the place. For instance when Mimi Jones and I met, she was walking in the opposite direction from me but on the same street near Downtown Crossing. She was coming from the Department of Motor Vehicles where she had paid off her son's parking tickets and I was on my way to the zoo with four temporary children from one family. I asked her if it was too far to walk as we both paused at a bus stop.

"It's far but you can do it," she said casting an accountant's glance at the children. "Wow," she said, "they're all the same age."
"It's okay," I told her. "Not quite."
"Really? Looks to me like you've got your hands full. I'll walk with you."

I thought her kindness might be a sign of insanity, but she was trimly dressed, tidily coiffed, lightly made up. Her

TWO SIDES OF A CRIB

complexion was a lovely tea tone, her face round and smooth but serious as if she contained innumerable bruises and soft spots in her feelings. She mosied along at my side pushing the bars of the three-person contraption with her hands beside mine. She told me about her son who was a Black Panther working a Free Breakfast program and about her other son who went all the way through law school, then dumped all that work to become a journalist.

"I know someone like that," I told her.

"It must be a trend then. I suppose you can use law for everything. He's not a hippy but he likes white people. Enough. His hero is Malcolm X. Heard of him?"

"Yes he sounds exactly like my friend," I said.

"My son? Well, It's generational. To want to break down artificial barriers. Your age group has done a great job already, beginning in the south. Now try the north."

We started up Blue Hill Avenue. It was autumn and the wind blew sticky papers and brown leaves around our legs. I wrapped my kids' faces in their scarves. "My name is Mimi. Mimi Jones."

"Jones. My friend's name is Jones."

"There are millions of us."

"Lewis Jones," I said swelling like tunnel vision at the utterance of his name.

"Lewis? That's my son," said Mimi.

We both stopped, gaping and clutching our faces, then nothing was spoken for many seconds until she hastily embraced me, hooked her arm through mine and we walked, stuck to each other, pushing the kids, and didn't stop talking for hours. Goats, chicks, hampsters, piglets and a pony later, we were seated on a bench with cigarettes and cokes making plans to meet there the next Saturday. Gravity was more like it. The pull down and into, against and onto, the thick leafy body of relationship. Children toddled, squabbled, giggled, petted animals, ate drank and rolled around while we told each other everything about ourselves but always returned to the heart, like hands grabbing a hot water bottle under the sheets, Lewis.

"When I am dead… they shall find your picture in my heart," John Donne raved to his beloved. I think Mimi understood that there was an agonic line between me and Lewis. It was an imaginary line connecting us though our declination was zero. Magnetics work at zero point. Magnetics can be gods or multiple gulps from the whole Logos.

Mimi understood power like this. She had warm dry hands and a tight grip. She had raised her boys in Lawrence, Kansas, then following Lewis, out came to Boston in the eighties. The father's sister Ruby was already living there. They were all except the father quite young. The father was a fat old man, a reverend genius, who had followers rather than a congregation. He had saved Mimi from the streets when she was fifteen, implanted his ancient seed in her twice, then became flaccid and celibate and a bookaholic with a mystical twist. All he did was read. She was only fifty to his seventy when I met her and glamorous in a surreptitious way, certainly immaculate like Libby. Those low-key sweet perfumes, fitted muted and soft clothes. She worked at the post office in Post Office Square and brought home the bacon to the old man hibernating in their basement apartment on Warren Street.

She never talked when she was at home. Her mouth clamped shut. She became cattish, slinking around taking care of cleaning and feeding and the younger son when he came home at night. The old man retained everything. He had a following by day, men and women who came to learn Sanskrit and Indian history that included Jesus as a wandering avatar. He especially loved Muktananda.

At the zoo she and I talked about God through the Upanishads. The Bhagavadgita, Plotinus, Dionysus, Weil, Dostoevsky, Tolstoi, etcetera, it was a full time preoccupation for those of us who had no childhood training.

Boston had called to the old man although he rarely walked down her streets but ordered others instead to bring him the books that rocked on steep stacks around his sagging sofa. You might have guessed he was gay because of the high timbre of his voice and his dramatic gestures, but Mimi said he had been her greatest lover and even his corpulence could not make her stop wishing he would do it again.

INDIVISIBLE

THE LIGHT OVER THE HEAVY DOOR

7-1

The apartment when I am up alone at night is lighted the way 1930's movies used to be when they showed dark rooms illuminated by a big white light from a tiny source. I can't make physical sense of this whiteness in the night room that faces the river. Only a distant streetlight. Other apartments gently shine behind drawn curtains. I think everyone else in the world except me is happy and in company. I know it. The enormous giant who inhabits this space with us we have dubbed The Bumper, and his head touches the ceiling, his shoulders slope. He would if he could burst into the space that divides heaven from earth, gush upwards dripping, naked and triumphant, the Purusha, an utterly enlightened embodiment of a fully realized human being, a feminine man luxuriant in hair and muscle, nearly red, both breasted and erect. The Bumper, however, is crushed and sad in the rooms we inhabit. Like so many losers and maniacs, his poor posture has always given him away.

7-2

There is a color that really has no name. I think also that there is one composed of a mix of silver and gold that can't be analyzed or faced because of its dazzle. Some heavy silver is where you see it sometimes. It is the color of Mimi's silence. Mabarosi, the Japanese call it when the silver sea-light sucks you back into itself. She said once: "I thought you were speaking of me." A strange sentence that made "I" into a reserved and watchful authority over "me" who was someone else entirely. She might as well have said, "I thought you were speaking of Mimi." She worked for society and was rewarded with a cell. In jail it is stupid to say that the cells are monkish because they are crowded. Three persons in one, each desiring freedom from the other. Mimi missed her husband who never once came to visit, but wrote her magnificent letters that the guards jeered at first. They were unsealed when Mimi finally received them and stained with coffee and the tear stains of laughter.

The Trinity in Greek and Latin has a feminine root.

Mimi said, "I knew that God was taking me seriously when he wouldn't let me have what I deserved. After all my work. This was the mark, the turning point. Others were being well rewarded for doing less. Including Lewis, my own son. There had to be a reason, and luckily I figured out what it was. I was being taken seriously."

During the early times with Mimi, there were assassinations and riots, and the city was cordoned off. At night it was like crawling across an anonymous floor in a pitch black room looking for a pine of light. Police cars and sirens playing "Break Up to Make Up." You expected the city to kill itself. I waited for Lewis out in my car on many nights during the riots. Why was I there and what did he need me for? To drive him here and there where he interviewed people and took pictures of things. My white face felt like something I had foolishly chosen to wear to the wrong place. Lewis was paranoid about being trailed so a white face helped. Sometimes he lay on the floor in the back seat. His parents' phone was bugged and tapped and the Feds were already following his brother while Mimi and the old man tried to keep him at home. We went from Connolly's to Bob the Chef to Joyce Chen's and the Heath Street projects. To Mission Hill and Fort Hill, Centre Street and Mattapan...

I lied to my husband telling him I was going to meetings down at the health clinic where I was on the board. He appreciated the lie. It meant I was scared. He would have been mad if I had told him I was helping Lewis because it would have meant I had no fear. He always said, "Just don't let me see you with him" – an order that had more to do with Lewis's looks than with mine. Sometimes I lay across the front seat in the car, listening to Motown play low, while Lewis was inside some building. I knew my maker, God, during those hours. Something that killed and was not killable. When I heard a door shut and Lewis's footsteps, I leaped up not wanting him to see me being a coward. How fat and ugly I felt goes without saying. All I did was take up space.

Every footmark that closed the space between us, that put him warmly in the closed car beside me, seemed to demonstrate a question of physics. I didn't believe in acts coming to meet my hopes yet there I lay waiting for his body to arrive, and it did. And I didn't believe in relativity, yet there I lay counting the scuffs in time to my heartbeats.

7-3

Tom dresses sloppily and works in the garden without gloves. He has a potential beard even after he has shaved, is hairy, thick and clumsy. He will never tell me about his sexuality, but says he doesn't like "too much man" in one place and this is his main problem with living in a monastery, and at the same time "gay is here to stay" as if he knows why. He wants to find a reason to condemn homosexuality but can't because it exists and always has. My feelings are hurt if I sense that he prefers men to women. He will only say that he would rather prefer women to men. God, I am sick of him. He makes me hate myself. His cool is unending even though he looks wild and passionate like an 18th century Russian ikon.

Some whites are secret blacks and some Jews are hidden Christians and some blacks are secret whites and some Christians are hidden Jews. Some children are old at heart and some old people are young. Lewis was like a hidden Jew who was black all the way through. He was like the missing page where the Old Testament meets the New. He had two sides to him – one being a fiery activist, the other a prophet of tragedy. When he first heard of my coincidental encounter with his mother, he just said "fuck" and went on doing his push-ups. But then he, being crooked like me, immediately took advantage of the situation and ordered me to accompany Mimi to Mass and to visit her every sunday when he couldn't be there. As a sign of the times, we were a negative, a minus, and a below zero.

He told me to do things I would have done anyway and then took credit for me doing them. We had many disagreements about politics, people, books, music, art but not movies. It was hard to figure out the essential ingredient that made a situation good for him. In the end I realized that it came down to him being a Catholic. Nothing, to him, that was extra was good. Only necessities and the givens were uncorrupted. Vanity to him was the motive behind almost every act and production, and so it was only the spontaneous or heart-driven that got past his suspicion. Then he would smile knowingly and nod his head, arms folded against his expansive chest. He wasn't my brother, son, husband, father or lover, but being present at his pleasure made me happy. It is out of such weakness that the warlike male is created.

Bricks frame my view from this seat and I think the water wants to be saturated like a cloth dragged through water the way it runs so lamely. But it's a dark and frigid day, all gold disgorged onto the tops of things, the rain has turned to snow and the river is fast and brown sticks are rigid against the ripple effect.

Mimi asked: "Which would you rather be when you die—the air or the earth?"
"Please, the water," I told her.
"And you?"

"We will never be ether," is what I think I heard her say. And then she remarked, looking away: "Henrietta, why are you the way you are?"

THE MIDDLE

When Henrietta was seven, and her father dead, she was brought before Judge Bumpers, a left-handed comedian who had worked in the court system for decades. He declared her mother incompetent to care for her and sent her to live with two old people who had prayed for a girl to be sent to them. They were vegetarian pacifists and had her sleep between them in their double bed. They were white from the tops of their heads to the tops of their feet. They ate a surplus of raw vegetables, lots of chocolates and rice and this became her preferred diet for life.

At seven Henny was cheeky and cute and liked adults to like her even as she wanted to be free of them. She simply wanted to be near to every person without being seen, and that was why so many of them said, "I don't remember her." She was as thin as a kitten with pointy features, black curls and soulful blue eyes. She wore big shoes and socks and knee-length dresses, her legs like stems too weak for their fronds and always some peculiar piece of clothing, or an accessory was added on to give her a certain feeling about herself. Candy necklaces, tiny pins shaped like animals, fake pink pearls, and oversized hand-knitted sweaters with parades of elephants or flowers woven into the chest, which she chose from piles at the Salvation Army with the old lady beside her.

She didn't miss her mother who was incarcerated both in a state mental hospital and inside her psyche. The one grandparent (her father's mother) she had was living in Ireland up near the border. Eckhart said of the soul, "In the desert of herself she is robbed of her own form, and in God's desert leading out of hers, she is bereft of name." This child believed her soul was alive inside her. "I see for something else. I eat for something else." She played with her soul instead of dolls. The old couple were kind to her, they paid for her to to go a private school nearby, and they watched her skittishness with affection. She didn't like them to touch her so deep was her sleep—hell wedged between those two decaying but live bodies that tossed and snorted like sea monsters.

She was fascinating to her more privileged schoolmates at the Mystic School. Her tragic history, her eccentric clothes, and the fact that she was silly all alone made her interesting. She didn't seem to care what anyone thought of her as she jump-roped in her enormous shoes. She even sucked her thumb in public with a blissful look in her blue eyes. Soon others discovered she could be fun, which is a great human trait.

Once Judge Bumpers came to her in a dream, his body filling the view she had of an ocean shining like the moonlight of the soul. And his shadowy form laughing shouted: "Aren't people awful? A complete disappointment.

And I made them!" He laughed warmly and engulfed her inner eye with his shadow so she had to wake up. She had a high fever and had to stay home from school. It turned out she had polio and the old couple had to drive her to a children's hospital. Once the nurses had to puncture her spine for fluid and they all held her down talking baby-talk and she learned irony from this arrangement – that those who cause the greatest pain, speak the kindest. The agony was incommunicable so she never mentioned it.

She learned to walk again with the other afflicted children but her legs were thinner than ever and she had an awkward posture for life. When she left the hospital and others in iron lungs and wheelchairs, she gulped down her grief at her good luck. Why live in such an unjust world if not to try to make things fair? For a year she had physical therapy with a woman who also massaged the muscles in her legs and leaned around her enveloping her in breath that was supernaturally light murmuring "angel" and "cookie" at her. Then she would go home to the old couple but now the man was hacking sick and dying. And soon she was left alone with the old woman who clung to her in bed so hard no one would believe it, not a social worker or a teacher at school, so she didn't try to tell them.

Only the physical therapist, who was also a nun, listened to something in her bones and assured her that she was not alone and that she would visit her once a week at home to make sure everything was all right. Sister John helped her to walk almost normally though she would never be exactly straight, her butt would stick out and her spine would curve in more than it should. She was still very thin and cheerfully played through her days at school, but at the center of her mind was Sister John who kept her promise about visiting her.

It wasn't long before Henrietta met Libby Camp at last. Libby was on the playground tar with her dress pulled tight by her little hands over her knees, its hems tugged down to her ankles so it looked like the plaid might rip around her knees. Libby had brown bangs lying over her eyebrows and a wide smile across tiny sharp teeth. She was bossy and riotously funny. From their first encounter on a May day in the playground, they were inseparable, their giggles preceding and receding around them. Or like two people performing the same religious rite, they seemed to move in unison.

Now the old lady grew ill from missing the old man and no matter how hard she squeezed the little girl she couldn't reinvigorate her own spirit. She began to decline. Sister John, who always had coffee in the kitchen with the old lady, noticed this and began arrangements for the child to be moved to a healthier foster family in a nearby town. The child howled, heaving her thin shoulders, her face between her skinned knees, saying she couldn't leave Libby.

Then Sister John taught her to pray and in the bathroom, they kneeled at the bathtub side by side, Sister's pink rosary beads clattering against the procelain and they said the Our

Father and Hail Mary nine times and begged Jesus to find a way for her to stay in her school.

Jesus did. Her mother was released from hospital and moved into a little brick flat near her school and the child was allowed to leave the old lady and go home. She was flooded with gratitude at being able to stay with Libby in school, and she never forgot the kindness of Sister John who went to Africa to teach, or the old lady who died in her sleep leaving her enough money to complete a private education through age twenty one. And Sister John didn't forget her, but sent her postcards for three years, and once told her about an English girl who became a nun but lived like an Indian, a boy named Julio and about a wounded gazelle. She lost and forgot these cards as the years passed.

"You may have settled your destiny with that one prayer beside the bathtub," Sister said.

Henrietta worried about her mother who changed her dread every minute. She was like a person you had to keep an eye on – a child for instance. Her mother had a worry M stitched into her brow, which she covered with black bangs, and her lips were circled with dark red lipstick. She called herself Creole and knew a few French words. She cleaned houses and offices for a living and listened to the radio. She was terribly tidy, but moved things back and forth a lot too. She had a special order for washing dishes (glasses first, cups next, cutlery last) and a special method for cleaning your bottom in the bathroom. She was in a perpetual state of insatiable desire which she fomented with alcohol. This way her eroticism was self-made but also required fuel which Henny was supposed to provide during the sober hours. Henny was asked to regale her with school stories, especially ones that showed how awful all her friends' parents were.

At home the child felt as if she was in a clay palace where she was deciphering shapes by touch. Her mother didn't seem to hear her or get her jokes.

Henny sucked her thumb until she was nine when Libby made fun of her, and she stopped. "Speak to my mouth if you want to talk to me but are afraid," a blind person might say, on being ignored. Henny often covered her mouth for fear of the effect her words might have, and how ugly her laugh might be. Burned toast was her favorite food. She left the bread in the toaster until it was smoking, then scraped off the black dust with a knife and ran her fingertips through the char, licking it off with the butter-grease. She also talked to Jesus for years even when she got smacked on the mouth for "nonsense" the day her mother heard her praying by accident.

She always wanted her mother to be happy but it was a futile business and soon her silence set in, the silence she was known for.

If a girl could develop her own ideas on the mysteries of the Torah, she might possibly have to be secretive about it and she would definitely have to be an obscure person.

There once was a shoemaker who stitched together the upper and lower worlds with his thread. He was an ordinary working man in a little shop in the Middle Ages. Sewing had a mystical edge to it, like arranging flowers and making tea.

Aristotle said that "woman has an extremely humid body, as can be known from her smooth and glossy skin, and especially from her regular purgations which rid the body of superfluous humors. So when wine is drunk and merged with female humidity, it loses its power and does not easily strike the seat of her brain when its strength is extinguished." The mother was without defenses and only confident when she had a drink in her hand when she jovially explained that she had a hollow leg, so the child once pretended she was an alligator crawling on the floor under her mother to see if her leg looked like a barber pole. But she saw a garter belt, skin, buckles and big salmon pink underdrawers. On those happy nights her mother played music and took giant-steps. The wet sexual implications of her excitement did not go un-experienced by her daughter, who felt herself to be a dangerous stimulus. But she was always put in a scared mood the next day which made gin the cause of her outbursts of bile and grief regarding human happiness, that same happiness that had been hers the night before. She hid in her closet and cried to God. She beat at the child's face and neck, it felt monkey-like, she pleaded, repented, swilled vodka and went back to work. A couple of her best jobs she got through her daughter's school – and one of which involved cleaning Libby's house twice a week. Henny always feared her mother would be

caught by the law and imprisoned again for being insane.
Women come in several forms like the ten names of the
Sefiroth, and for each form there is its opposite – wisdom
becoming stupidity, intelligence becoming intolerance,
good humor turning to hate, fun turning to fury, etcetera.

Meantime the two girls were constantly switching forms
between themselves, until graduation, and for them the
search for truth was not active or passive but nervous.

The maid's daughter was aware that good things had
unfolded for her out of trouble. She had a good school, and
a best friend, neither of which would have occurred if it
hadn't been for her mother's breakdown, the old lady's
kindness and her sickness leading to the nun's attention.
Likewise she never could drain from her cells the scent of
Sister John's gentle breath, the stench of the old lady, her
mother's likkerish laugh which all all combined later into
the fragrance of Libby's bitter weed.

She grew into a slightly bow-backed hard-assed woman on
two pin legs. Her walk was a bit stiff as if she had ridden a
horse for the first time every day of her life.

Her expression was farouche, her mouth sensuous and
small until it opened into a huge smile that creased her
cheeks. A rare bird, weird. The best thing about her was two
large eyes which held the luminous wonder of a baby. She
and Libby spent some afternoons at Libby's house, the
intensity of their friendship was a secret from their

classmates, and sometimes her mother moved around them vacuuming and blasting Edith Piaf or Tchaikovsky on the record player. Like many women, Henny would never surpass her mother economically or socially, though her mind would travel to much farther, and worldlier places.

Adolescence has its own literature which will not be represented in these pages, but the history of a head is unavoidable being everywhere.

The snaky gray brain that doctors and scientists dump and slice and slap their hands around, chop, dice and analyse outside and inside its hard shell case, is not much to look at it. And you can't look into it, in the normal sense of seeing more. You only see less than enough, every time. Where are all those pictures being made? And why cry out of such a clay? Ephraim, a Syrian father, said that until you have cried, you do not know God. And some holy men wanted tears to be a sacrament. The body, Ayurvedic healers tell us, contains its own cures. We have what we need. Incredulous are those who figure out that the Interior Life is simply the activity of human cells.

Having a relationship that begins with the ownership of a body and ends with the owner wondering who the owner is who is owning whatever it is that can't be owned, is peculiar enough. But having another body under your moving hands, crying "My turn!" or "Do whatever you want with me!" is even more peculiar.

However, knowing that it is peculiar is the really peculiar thing, because that knowledge indicates an awareness of a perfect being somewhere – perhaps even a good being against whom we measure all our qualities.

THE END OF THE MIDDLE

A VAULT WITH A RED STAIN

8-1

Some doctors inspect the brain as if each melody were a malady. They want to find the origin of song as if it were a clay reed that would play without breath. But the doctor who lived in the little border town near the compound was not reductive or materialist. We went to ask her about the boy we had lost in the canyon. Had a sick child come in? Where might he have gone? We were all standing in the parking lot outside her adobe office.

She was a woman with a plain long-lipped face in yellowish hair, she looked like a broken harp. Yet there was an intensity of compassion in her that was fruitful under the circumstances.

Her name was Kerry and she came from the forthright if eccentric Berkshires. She said, "Don't be surprised by anything you find out about children here. They get lost, they get raped, they get cut up for body parts, they get picked up by the INS.... He probably just wandered back to his campsite. These heavy rains always turn up ugly things," she said. "It's as if they wash off the top and what's underneath – well, you wish you didn't know it was there."

It was like finding meteor pebbles in the sole of your sneaker. Tom and I both felt sick and kicked at the tar. The doctor's drabness was a function of her selflessness, how I admired her! She had no time for herself and didn't even eye a cookie in a nearby window.

In *The Revelation of the Veiled*, Hujwiri says, "There are three forms of culture: worldly culture, which is the mere acquisition of information; religious culture, which means following rules; and elite culture which focuses on self-development."

There are also veils over nationalism, no one speaks of them, especially the ways in which the elite in their drive for individual power are feeding the military dogs they despise. Personal ego is the most precious bullet in the nation's arsenal!

The doctor said, "The sale of, well, the commodification of the human body, is as old as prostitution and slavery. I've got to go, but I'll tell you if I hear anything about where this poor kid came from. The other thing is, there is a place that takes battered kids and places them in foster care. I mean, you might locate him there."

"But something more humane? Are there nuns – orphanages?" Tom asked.

"There are," said the doctor, "on the other side of the border. But first take a look at this other place, way east. Desert. I mean, if you want to bother. But really I suggest just letting it go. He's probably fine."

"I hope so," said Tom and glanced at my silence.

"I had a really confused childhood," the doctor suddenly announced as she moved to her car, "in upper state Massachusetts. I never thought I'd be a doctor – just a nurse, a caretaker. But the men made me so mad. So I went to med school.

"Tom's head went inside her car window. "It's great you can do so much good."

"Good? You're a priest, right?"

"No, I'm between things, you might say."

"Oh, one of those," she said bitterly. "So why are you here?" Tom looked as if he had been hit, but replied evenly: "Well, Henny and I came here together. The place belongs to her, and we just wanted to see, you know, uh, take a break."

She stared clear-eyed at his morose expression, obviously wondering if we were having sex together there. "A break from what?"

"From, we have some things, to think about," he said.

"Why not turn that place into a sanctuary?"

"For?"

"You don't know?" she asked and gunned her engine. "Women? Kids? Illegals?"

"All of those and more... Why not?" And then she roared away in her car, when she was ready to do so. No hovering or polite goodbyes. Tom had never looked more wounded by words.

8-2

"You can tell if a blind person is really blind if he can't smell a freshly baked cookie under his nose, someone told me," the superintendent said. "But I don't understand how." He wanted me to tell him about blindness, but I wouldn't.

He had fixed the lights in the building but now the elevator didn't work. An old lady was almost in tears, not knowing how to get to the fourth floor where her apartment was. It was around eight p.m. I asked her if she could climb a few stairs at a time, then rest, etcetera, and I told her I would go with her. She said she supposed she must and took my arm thinly. We climbed the back stairs in silence except for gasps. The usual question that arises in such conditions came into my mind: "Why live for this long?" The old lady was a frail wheezing dependent being, unwanted by anyone in the world (she told me this on the third floor) except a nephew who was impatiently waiting for her to die and leave him her money. "I don't know why I go on," she squeaked and stood still, clinging to me and the bannister, all but keeling over. "Well, yes, I do… To make that boy wait until it's too late for him to enjoy my money."

"Why not just leave it to some charity instead?"

"I don't trust charity. And he's adopted. I dislike giving him the family money. He can have it when I don't know. Why should he have it anyway, just because my sister took him in? Our society has lost its direction, I tell you, too many people. We should celebrate every time there is an earthquake and a war that kills more people. My nephew has no class, no taste, no matter how much my sister did for him. It's in his blood. I know you aren't supposed to say it but breeding makes all the difference."

She then began her final ascent up the metaphor of stairs. "There's an awful racket in the pipes here. Banging night and day like Samuel Whiskers. Have you heard it? Think it's a rat? Should we report it? I didn t respond. At her apartment door I waited while she fumbled for her key, let herself in, fumbled for the light, and banged shut the door without a backward glance or thank you. The Japanese are said to have tossed a load of Vietnamese boat people back into the sea when they didn't thank them for picking them up. But certain Buddhist teachers advise you to use all negative encounters as lucky lessons.

Down below in my white room I remember Mimi while listening to a tape of Mozart's Quintet in G, my chair tilted to the left to point out at the straw-gold lines over the river. There is no sound from the closet down the hall – not a bump or a snore or a child's humming.

I think Plotinus noticed that enlightened people don't need to remember the past. Re-configuring days or minutes is of course impossible but, God, remember Proust had rats delivered to his room so he could torture them. I don't believe in the unconscious, because whatever it is, it is not un-anything. That watery junk that floats through and around my bones is alive and well and near the tops of things, by no means under or reactionary. Why, dreams luxuriate in sheets and pillows and night all around them as if the head is a bed. If I am lucky Libby will swim by today, waving from a day that does not dwell in my unconscious but in the most wakeful part of my cerebellum.

8-3

The Gita Chapter 12: "Concentration is better than mere practice, and meditation is better than concentration; but higher than meditation is surrender in the love of the fruit of one's action, for on surrender follows peace."

Jesus is said to be a fisher of men and his hook and line fly into time and draw you to him. The pin digs in but only after you make the choice to bite.

The Gita wants the best for the reader. You can tell because of the many choices it offers unlike some cruel and dogmatic systems. It is written without judgment. If you can't meditate, concentrate. Or as Teresa says, "If you can't contemplate, recollect." Some people say it is enough to live seriously or to become "Zero at the Bone." But Keats wrote in a letter that our lives have a transcendent value that we can't apprehend. I think the way they talk about God as "love" is a heresy unless the word "love" has no meaning but then all words about God have to have less meaning than the word God itself which, because it already has no meaning at all, places all words in a difficult situation.

So why do they blow God into a word that is stuffed with meaning if it makes us all feel sick?

8-4

Through heavy drug-use, through child-bearing and rearing in a halfhearted reckless way, through sex with strangers and on, Libby continued meditating. Her stare then was like a beetle seated at the edge of a forest, and if a stone flew past, the beetle didn't see it. One true gaze into such an empty pair of eyes and your life is changed. "Whose sin was it that caused his blindness?" someone asked Jesus about a poor blind man. His answer was a reproof: "If you were blind there would be nothing wrong with your failure to see what's going on. But you do see and still you don't get what's happening."

What is a tea-person? Is it a person who meditates over the tea ceremony? When Libby was having her tea in my house and sleeping with McCool, I was given by fate the consolation prize of my friendship with Mimi.

McCool and Libby had each other and I had Lewis's mother and prematurely snow white hair.

My friendship with Mimi lasted many years that included the development of four to six children into their teen years, and her youngest son Walk into manhood. As planned, she never saw me and Lewis at the same time.

Mimi's apartment was lit electrically all day. Table lamps with weary shades gave the place a nearly occult glow. Books on the floor, the tables, beside the john, at the kitchen table. Some photographs of old family members were hung lopsidedly, the furniture was thrift shop but comfortable. It always held the lovely childhood smell of toast throughout its rooms. It was a floor-through with a big bed for Mimi and Pop and in the other room twin beds for the boys though Lewis hadn't ever slept there. He was the household hero. Mimi collected all clippings of his writings.

Walk was the one Mimi suffered over. He was born much later than Lewis – one of those children who should be a grandchild – but he was the son she loved like a mother. He went AWOL in the army, dropped out of correspondence high school, ended up in a Columbian jail for carrying marijuana, all before the age of twenty. He was a guitarist, gifted, good at languages, in these he was his father's son. Walk was not as good-looking as Lewis, but he had more friends, was kinder, funnier, more artistic, and better to his mother. He practiced yoga and had an intense but eccentric religious intention that kept switching allegiances.

With Walk and Mimi the deep needle began its in-and-out movements through the tapestries pricking and drawing spouts of blood.

Walk came and went daily. He was stocky with a slight speech defect (a twist to his lips) that made him appear amused by all he observed and gave others the impression that he was always joking. So no matter what he said people laughed. It was as if he had been labeled a comedian after making one good joke. The punishment was, it was hard to take him seriously. He wore pleated workpants and a blue workshirt and a khaki army jacket. His friend Jimmy was a big frightened boy who married very young and let himself be bossed around. Heaven was his other friend, a tall mixed race boy who had traveled from somewhere south of New York City, who played bass, read a lot, and seemed dreamy like his name but in fact he was sharp, alert, and full of plans. Pop thought Heaven was gay and Heaven thought Pop was gay and called Mimi Ma.

Once I arrived home too quickly and too early for my husband and Libby to pretend they were just friends and be prepared. I sort of planned it like that. What I saw was the same as what I would get watching a blocked television channel where sex is coming through the wobbling ruptures, cheap music playing like bars. I hovered beside the door. My most beloved friend, a slip of a woman, was being fed on by McCool with his black hair torn at the roots by her two brown hands and two of them sounding as if they were in hell. Downstairs boiling tea my shoulders shook, but I felt nothing. The steam from the kettle rinsed my face and I let it whistle and left the house to pick up the children. When I came home, Libby and my husband were drinking Lipton fully clothed at the kitchen table. They each smiled wearily at me as if I was a victor who might extend kindnesses to them, my prisoners. This was not far from the truth since they only wanted my happiness to come through theirs.

Luckily I understood that Libby meant well – in the sense of needing to justify herself – by trying to take my husband away so I could focus on Lewis in peace. McCool, on the other hand, was possessed and had no ulterior motives. He adored Libby. He was out of his mind with love. And now he encouraged my contacts with Lewis (once he had threatened to kill him) in an ingratiating self-serving way. McCool might ask: "Where's your old friend Lewis? Still living at home? Is that why you go over there all the time? Well, go, go, go. Enjoy yourself!"

He himself was a handsome man with bright blue eyes, fierce lines in his cheeks, red lips, black hair and a seething smile. He was charm itself, jumping up to fix a drink for you, kissing the children suddenly, telling hilarious stories when he wasn't ranting on about corruption in everyone but himself. He read a lot, remembered and quoted it, loved to hang out and not work except at his music. It took someone quite astute in human personality to notice the paranoia behind the kindness and the murder in his hysterical laughter. Libby certainly didn't notice these or need to. He was in love and wanted her only to know him as good. And she must have drained off some of the agony that made him twist and burn. He was actually soothed into a kind of honesty with Libby. McCool talked about race as if it was a disease. "He's smart, but black," he might say about someone we knew.

Pop would not let the subject of race arise under his roof. "This is a race-free zone," he said of his home and told how he had seen households poisoned by this subject all his life. He said, "Words will let you know, faster than any gesture, when a social issue is a psychosis. Race is a national psychosis, and I know it, because they can't fix a name for it. What are we? Black? Colored? Negro? Non-white? Minority? Of color? That's the worst of the lot, a sentimental slipshod phrase – 'of color'! Think about it. When the word fails, the idea is dead."

He was genuinely upset and lay down turning his back on all of them. Sometimes he listened to tapes spoken in Sanskrit, because it gave him peace of mind. Lewis said his father was not so much misunderstood as unable to express his ideas clearly.

Lewis recalled: "When I asked Pop what he thought about love, he said 'Live Time' in a jive voice and laughed. 'You mean like Live Music? Saturday Night Live?' I asked him and he nodded, still laughing from the belly up."
"But I think it makes sense," I said in such a low voice, Lewis didn't hear me.

8-5

They put on a nightmare for me. My own waste was splashed across my lower body. It was so bad, the doctor said, "No more theater for you, young lady." And I was horrified because just now Tom had accepted me as I was and didn't want me to be a stiff socialite (or socialist?) after all. What if he saw me like this? I would want to die. So instead I rushed away from the nightmare into the fog. I used this as the first part of a 13-minute video called *This Shit*.

8-6

Libby and McCool were so generous, they always stopped the car to buy something for someone they were visiting. "Whenever you visit someone, one arm should be longer than the other," McCool would say in his Dublin accent. But Libby had to be stoned no matter where she was going. And so McCool was useful to her because he cheated, stole, knew crooks, never paid his debts and lied his way out of all his troubles.

On the other side, he gave everything he had away, threw money at anyone who asked for it, stopped to help people in trouble, and knew how to fix a car. He always justified his petty criminality with weak politics that were all about despair and opinion and nothing involving risk and sacrifice, yet his life was all about risk and sacrifice. His debts lay far and wide, cutting a swath through pub after pub and restaurant after restaurant and bookstore after bookstore across the city. He was able to sustain this situation by his own acts of generosity.

He had a recurrent suspicion that I had saved Lewis's illegitimate children through foster care. "Because they all look like resurrected half-breed slaves," he explained. "I just bet that hack writer of a friend of yours has reproduced plenty." Yet he cared for the children tenderly and well.

Libby took him away to the Mexican border where her early husband had left her that crippled lot of huts on a canyon gold with nasturtiums. It was a deserted compound that might have been inhabited at one time by hippies or a cult Birds flew out of its windows as soon as they flew in.

To St. John of the Cross, memory is an obstacle to spiritual progress. To someone else serious, memory is the way God enters the brain. I was left with the children in a big stone house I couldn't afford on a small park in Roxbury. I was the only white person living there. Another one had been burned to death with gallons of kerosene. She was a young lesbian liberal who ran screaming for help. Who could forget this story? Especially not one living being hated. One after another people who were not white moved in with us – Jimmy and his wife, Heaven, then Mimi's husband's sister Ruby who helped with the children, and soon I had nothing to fear about being there. Not only were my foster children an indecipherable skin tone, I was white-haired and plain. I went to work part time as a photographer for the city's one black newspaper, and then moved into documentary and editing, making short films of an educational nature, about safety belts and drugs. Here I began a 20-year project, a film made of the unused ends of others' reels. And I made little videos from my dreams.

Years passed other years, the children left home, and my family was made up of a circle of old friends.

At one point Walk was driving Mimi insane. "You're a waste of time, just like my brother, a total loser, I can't look at you without crying…" And he responded, "Look at you, slaving day and night, all your life, at a dead-end job and living in a dump. What's to be proud of? Obeying the law?" And then he slammed out and I stayed behind. Mimi was trembling but close-mouthed. We went into the kitchen, a wood and linoleum affair, always immaculate, and put the kettle on. Mimi drank Maxwell's instant coffee with evaporated milk. I steamed on about the mystery of the words, "Lead us not into temptation" which sounded to me as if they were addressed to the devil rather than God.

8-7

"You are always welcome to use the chapel as a sanctuary for prayer. Please consult the schedule for the brothers' round of worship and prayer." Here where the brothers live under the Rule of Life are granite walls, undressed slate floors, Belgian marble walls and roof beams torn from the old Mystic River Bridge. I like the way they have Mary here holding the child and wearing a sapphire blue robe and a crescent moon is beneath her, golden spikes come from her person pointing up to the twelve stars that circle her head. Nearby angels swing their censers and sing. That's where I pray, under the Rose Window, to be a worker who can stir the heart of Mary to intervene and bring peace to the world.

If you say her name, she looks to God for a response. Is there irony in heaven? The Roman Centurions knew irony and so did the Greeks, but did the saints when they were performing extreme acts of penance? I think they wanted to be crushed into bars of pure God. Irony marks the end of the year. It wears the face of an accountant who is adding things up that were never meant to connect.

I learned to think as I went along reading, listening, dreaming, filming, sometimes auditing a lecture somewhere, then I rushed home to my children and the gravity of the kitchen sink.

Lewis was epiphanized in all these people, blood relatives and friends. What is suzerainty without a real body to fill its shoes. Hidden feelings yearn to be heard and so our heart-words called out to Lewis, through all of this, Love us! If Mimi formed the center of his world she now formed mine too, so there we met. However, the vulva-shape made by overlapping circles is no safer than a full shape floating on its own proportions – squares, ovals, rectangles. Everyone pretended they were safe. Since all dying is a kind of murder by this world, I would like to be able to declare, "I served another world." Just to have been true to one desire would have been enough for me, the rest of it all is so confusing.

In accordance with the wishes of friends, family and white racists, no one saw Lewis and me together, not even Libby, so we were like two living underground in separate rooms but calling. Now I can thank God we were never lovers or I would have lost him. Then I suffered because I believed we were victims of our times.

One time he told me: "I have one regret…. No child… I wish I had had a child. I even put some of my sperm on ice, in case I got too old, or ill – and look at me now. Lucky I did."

"But you'll have to find a surrogate mother, if that's what they're called."

"Suffragette. Ha ha. And what does it really mean?" he asked. "I think we are all genetically identical over the long haul. I mean, in one lifetime you have individual characteristics and tendencies, but all humans have the same ingredients generally – dementia, schizophrenia, bad eyesight, cancer, heart disease, rotten teeth – just a difference in quantity."

"So what you're saying – "
"Is that I should have just adopted some needy kid years ago. It would've been the same as having my own."
"I know," I agreed.
"You would. You did. You took care of strangers but I bet you wish you'd had your own."
"Of course."
"Why didn't you just dump McCool, or come to me?"
"You didn't ask me, Lewis."
"McCool should feel really guilty."
"So what. He thinks you have fathered scores of children."
"Why did you stay with him. I always wanted to ask."
"Because I, well, you, in a way."
"Don't blame me!"
"I can't explain it."
"There you go, swallowing your words."

"I felt sort of sorry for him.

"So?"

"Well, we both got into the kids. And loved them. It seemed like fate."

"Bullshit."

"What?"

"You didn't want them yourself."

"Why not?" I asked Lewis.

"You don't dare love. Your mother was insane, I don't know. But I think O'Cool was perfect because you don't love him and not having your own kids was perfect because you might love them too intensely if they were yours. You love people you can't have. Believe me. I understand that one. Only too well. Only too well."

"But you came from a stable adoring family."

"It made me arrogant. I thought I was immortal for way too long. Now I'm fucked up in a fucking wheelchair, childless, like a baby, useless."

"I'll take care of you."

"Push another infant around? Thanks but no thanks. Enjoy your freedom. You've paid your dues."

Crushed, I pushed at the arms of my seat, getting ready to go. "Where are you going?" he asked.

"Home."
"Do you need taxi money?"
"No way."

Hot behind the eyes, I left him there. At a movie theater, parked in the middle of the aisle. We had just seen *Forbidden Games*, watched the credits through to the end, in the empty afternoon theater.

8-8

It wasn't much later when Lewis's father said: "Those born before the war believed in manners and forms, recognizable gestures that showed social differences between people to be as intractable as caste differences.... social as in having to do with education, generation, experience, and money. They were polite. Now our children judge us and are rude, but honest. They exploit and belittle their elders. And they justify all this by their infantile politics." Pop ranted while Walk yawned. "The problem," Mimi said, "was never what we couldn't have, ourselves, but what we haven't done for each other. This is what we can't face. A communitarian failure."

Walk moaned a yawn and his father snarled, "Get on out of here." So he left for the kitchen, leaving Mimi to return to her happy silence while the old man snoozed over a copy of *The Cloud of Unknowing*. I was there but the hour seemed insignificant. Retrospect is sequence. Sometimes you would be in Mimi's house, lose her for a few minutes, then find her sprawled across the belly of the old man breathing him in as if he were her baby and him stroking her with his two soft hands, a book slid to the floor, him humming to her some song.

Then you would back out of the room and leave by the kitchen door. Ruby and I had this happen to us and we remembered it together because there was something in the shape they made circled in the gloom and the stacks of books that reminded us of the way certain paintings have oil so thick it is a smear off the natural, so unreadable close up and then so readable from afar, that it is like learning to see for the first time, figuring out the perspectives and spaces between objects.

Ruby and I loved to go to the Museum with the teenage children on its free afternoons and look at the Impressionists, the American Wing and contemporary art, so we saw lots of actual postures as paintings where we learned all we needed to know about color and content. Walk came with us twice. Ruby wanted him to go back to school, a community college would do. But he used the excuse of having no money to resist her. "I can contribute," Ruby said.

"And I can find it," his mother insisted. Mimi didn't rest when Walk was out of the house or when he was in it. She watched his every move, wondered where he got the little money he had from working playground duty in an after-school program down the street.

"Where did you get that ten?"

"I earned it, Ma. Remember?"

"You spent what you earned already."

"How do you know? You haven't got radar vision."

"I know what you earn and I have vision enough to see what you spend... Son, you better not be involved. You don't want to end up doing shut-in after all. It's hell in there."

"No, I know I don't, not ever."

"So watch it, son. Pop is not too well. You might need to go to the library for him."

"Don't worry. And I'll be going back to school soon too."

"To study what?"

"Music."

Walk played his guitar in the kitchen and sang the blues. She cleaned up around him and began to prepare a macaroni cheese and spinach casserole they all liked.

One Sunday Mimi took me into her room to look inside her deep dark wooden closet stuffed with shoes and clothes. We sat on her double bed which was covered with a quilt handmade by a friend in Lawrence, Kansas, a woman whose grandfather had been white and a slave. The quilt was stiff, heavy and geometrical in design. Red and yellow patches were sewn together with thick yellow thread. There was a cane chair in the room and an oak desk and dresser, plain white cotton curtains shut out the brick view. Books all over the right side of the bed which sagged lower than the left. Water guttered over the window panes. Mimi wanted my advice about criminal behavior because I was white, and she perched on the sagging side of the bed with her face turned toward the window where reflecting shadows off the water then gathered onto her cheeks. At the same time I looked at a picture of the family still in Missouri, many years before, and yearningly scrutinized Lewis young and athletic in his country clothes.

Mimi explained: "I think Walk has hidden some stuff in my closet. But I don't dare look."
"Stuff?"
"I don't know, just something illegal. There's a box back there."
"For how long?" I asked.
"About six weeks, six times, don't tell."
"What are you going to do?"
"He wouldn't do that, would he? I mean, hide it in his mother's closet!"
"It seems like the perfect place to hide it – to me," I said.

Mimi rubbed her eyes and scrutinized me who in turn scrutinized the photograph of Lewis with my hand shading off the place where the reflection of rain suddenly blocked my view of him.

"I don't dare look. But I don't want to know. Will you look?"

The closet door increased its depth by yards as I stood up to face it. Square darkness, square air. Clothes hanging neatly in rows and shoes stacked behind against the wall.

A closet is a kind of hole, its walls are floors. You want to crawl or enter on tiptoe. The fact is, a closet is equivalent to a corner of the brain where you hide the day's self-images. No one goes fully inside a closet but stands back and gingerly picks out an article of clothing, as if it was a cluster of fruit hanging on a bee-buzzing vine. "It's way in back, on the left," Mimi said.

I turned wonderingly, because she was so complex, so surprising to me. A mother. She couldn't face what Walk was really doing, even while she was monitoring his every move. Simone Weil suggested that the escalation of violence occurs because the victim imitates the tactics of the victor. I think the escalation of passivity occurs when a person fears for another person so deeply she can't move.

I was repelled by the closet – its black atmosphere was solid – when I glanced in the mirror across the room and saw myself large and blowsy, not the way I felt I looked (black-curled and childish). "I don't know," I sighed, it was now an agonized sigh. "It seems kind of…"

"I know," she said, face in hands. "Don't do it then. Let's leave it."
My attention had drifted up from my chest to my face. "I mean…. Well…"
"What's that?" Mimi was beseeching. It was a kind of falling, my evasion of her urgency – a yawn, a nod and a

swallowing down into space.

Mimi stared at me waiting, then said: "I feel so sorry for
him. He has this heroic brother. What's he to do. He can't
live up. He suffers. He has talent, lots of it, abilities, but his
ego is crushed by – well, you know who, and Pop too. They
look down on him. I want to help him, that's all, fifteen
hundred a semester, not a big deal."

"Won't Ruby?"

"Help? Yes, but he doesn't want that. He says she'll make
him pay in some way. She's so judgmental."

"But it's safer."

"No, I know."

Her collar lay red and open, a V across her chest, where I
could see a pulse operating in the little impression at her
throat. "I'm immobilized. I feel so sorry for him. What do
you think?" I was afraid to say that I felt the police were
already in the room with us, that Walk was someone who
had bad luck, that she should pull it out and flush it down
the toilet that minute. "I feel sorry for him too. Let's just risk
it."

Afraid it might pop the bubble in our thinking, I made
some joke, backed away from the closet, went home and
heard by word of Lewis's mouth on a breezy May day that
Mimi had been arrested and put in the Federal prison to
await trial for drug-trafficking. She was fifty four years old.

Lewis called to tell me. "Did you know about this?"

"Of course not," I lied.

"Motherfuckers came into the house and took her away in cuffs," he said, his voice shaking. "Why the fuck would she have dope? Was it my little asshole brother's fault? I just don't get it. Henny, I'm going crazy, but I'm going to do all I can, all I can. I'm going to do all I can to get her out.... Listen. Never let anyone you know – ever – go to prison. Promise? Promise."

There are studies on philosophies of subjectivity, using the example of a witness to an accident. In this example, the witness is passively involved in the accident by the mere fact of seeing it.

There are four attitudes a witness might take in regard to the event: one is to testify boldly in court to everything he or she saw; another is to avoid causing further chaos by saying "I don't really remember;" a third is to laugh with certain skeptics who have wondered, "Justice? Impossible in such a world!" and back away; and a fourth is a parody of the first. In this case the cynical witness testifies with embellishments, exaggerations, lies, just for the fun of it.

A fifth example is unmentioned but it is almost the same as the third. In this example, the witness finds a way to save the defendant from going to jail because she feels she caused the accident just by being there to observe it. She is so conscious of the causes and contingencies that brought her to that place, at that hour, she knows that she is responsible for its outcome. It is wonderful how nothing works.

Who said, "It is an odd domain, this 'inner' country, this invisible and silent place where revolutions take place before news of them gets out." I think the soul is a possession of the person and not a part of the person. It is like a baby you carry around and give to it whatever you can so it will know good. But does your soul have to love you in order to stay with you? And will it leave you if it stops loving you?

"Yes, yes, it will leave you. Definitely it will leave you," said Tom.

WISHING AROUND THE EDGES

9.1

Whenever I visited Mimi in prison I found her dressed in a crisp greenish uniform just like the other women wore, but Mimi looked elegant in it, just because of her posture and gesture. She always wore earrings which she rubbed between her fingers nervously.

Or else, seated, she leaned forward and pressed her hands in mine for the entire two hour visit. She was very thin and her complexion had developed something like stains. She always said, "I made a terrible mistake. I couldn't face reality."

Once early on she introduced me to people around. She did so with a low voice that gave me the impression that she was participating in their bad luck. A morose man with a beautiful boy under his hand and a wild-haired woman at whom the man never once glanced. She even introduced me to the guard who was a pretty Puerto Rican woman.

I was understood to be an aging beatnik and over a month of Sundays we all got comfortable with each other. Mimi wanted to hear details about my collection of children and hers. She liked to know about the weather outside and the animals at the zoo where she missed the birds especially. Mimi said her idea of paradise now would be to sit in the birdhouse and look and listen.

Walk had left the country with his money. Lewis visited his

mother whenever he could, the old man never did because he feared he would die if he saw her there.

And now the old man would not let me into the house. He abandoned his idea of his home as a race-free zone and became on the contrary obsessional about the betrayal by whites. Ruby, standing on one crutch with her neck thrust forward, and her eyeglasses flashing tinny circles, told me all about it. She said race was all anyone talked about in Pop's house as if Mimi, in fact, had been the one holding the subject at bay. One night stones shattered the windows in my house and this action seemed part of all the rest, Mimi in jail and the old man's rage and the city at large, and I knew I had to move my skin to another part of town. I was laughing when I left. There was lots to laugh about. My house was sold for six times the amount we bought it for. Reagan was President.

One winter day Lewis came to jail at the same time as me, and I waited in the lobby until he had finished with his visit. Outside he told me about the people there, as if I had never met them.

Lewis reported: "That fine woman Gemma is in for life. So soon there won't be anyone to take care of her kid. The guy really wants to get on with his monastic vows. You can imagine. It's not even his child. Or so he says."

As Lewis told me this I imagined him whirling himself around to look at the group collected around a sticky table because "That's one beautiful child," he said to me outside. "Blind or not." I groaned and moved away from Lewis, abruptly, and went to line up with the people entering. But he called after me: "Why the fuck didn't we just go and do it, Henny? Have a kid together, anything. I mean, fuck." I started to turn back but was pushed forward into the little chamber with the heavy locked doors.

Inside, breathless, I told Mimi what he had said to me. "I don't know why he never had a child," said Mimi. "It's what he needs, even this late. He needs a real home. Even that priest over there seems to have had a child."
"Priest?"
I found myself examining Tom. There was no scent but a kind of heat around his person that I suddenly wanted to partake of. I envied him for believing in God. I wanted to sit beside him for a long time. And I was still under the spell of Lewis, as if I had brushed under a rainy branch and the drops still glittered on my clothes, in my hair.

"I'm going to go talk to them," I told Mimi.

The boy's eyes were closed and his expression alert, and he had a small but eager smile on his lips. As ever his eyes were ringed with shadows, his lids heavy and his mouth was full and pink. "Gnomes again?" I asked. His mother moved back to make room for me, and I could see that she loved him objectively but without the swallowing attention that mothers who live with their children have.

Tom smiled at me, weakly, and murmured, "Gnomes." I had felt some tie between us already forming on visiting days, because we often eyed each other, then looked away quickly as if sickened. Now it was not strange for me to plant myself beside him even though we had had only a few conversations, mostly standing in line for our credential check, or while stuck in the little room waiting to be let into the prison area officially. He glanced sideways at me with a curt nod and read my mind. "We should talk outside of this place sometime," he said.

9-2

I see what's coming but I don't see where it's coming from. Every face and step is pitching forward only to be gone missing. The plaza showed it. Sky a bakery, each tree on the ledge. Libby and my husband left me that mildewed love nest on the border. The buildings they built plus the kitchen on legs that Tom and I painted. We went there together only months after Mimi left for Missouri. We stayed there longer than planned because we were happy that we hated it. Eat and run little birds, pink hibiscus orange and red nasturtium, a jacaranda that grows blue, bougainvillea like butterflies, neon pink or nearly brown and eucalyptus silver blue and bittersweet to smell. Everywhere the monkey-like idea of palm silhouettes, banana-skins and a coat over cream. Sitting outside at night was like passing around a razor to shave a zebra down to its first shape. The black sky is really a weight, can hurt, so heavy a dump of stars, some falling all turning together bare naked between them. God planted the glass that grew language.

"Sand, glass, they're the same thing," said Tom into the dark. "Do you really think that your Julio Solito is the same one as mine?"

"He has to be the same. There can't be two."

"It makes me think there really is a big plan, or pattern."

"Well, isn't that what you always think, as a priest, or monk, or whatever you want to be?"
"All I do is try to stay on the side of belief," he said. "My doubt is enormous."

"Apparently not as big as mine. Mine is the foundation of my hope that one day I might find God. If I didn't doubt so intensely, there would be no hope for me.... By the way, Blessed are they that mourn for they shall be comforted. What do you think that means?"

"I think the deeper you go, the safer it gets.... Plus I think he means that mourning helps you cross out of the world, unlike other emotions that really take you nowhere.... Lust, and so on."

Rain again gurgling and bubbling around my dreams and I swimming in the water around the hut, it turned corners and created former streets, deep green, clean water that boats began to use and pollute as I swam along calling for

Libby to come on down, leave her parents alone, and swim with me. And when she did she was finally smiling and happy because she couldn't hear them fighting anymore. She was dead or something.

9-3

When McCool returned from the border in the eighties, he came right to the house to reclaim me and the children. "I was only joking," were his first words to me. By then he and Libby had satisfied their curiosity about each other – or at least she had – and we had moved to a new neighborhood with people of all colors. Ruby lived with us still, Mimi was at home, and Lewis was always away. Cards from him in Jordan, Pakistan, Northern Ireland, Capetown. McCool got furious when he found them in my brown jewelry box tied up in a cliche-riddled ribbon. I wanted him to leave the house as a mouse, dead in a box. He stamped around raving about my obsession with Lewis and how women never wait for their men anymore but dream of others like troubadours. He compared me to a rabbit saying I would inherit the earth because I lived in a hole. All of us cried, the children and me, and begged him to leave. Then when he left, we sat down and ate a chicken pie voraciously.

With McCool there was no balance. When we met in the bar in 1970, I was sewing a dress for my mother who would only wear one style in a variety of patterns made by me. A-line below the knees, belted waist, buttons up to the neck, and a little middy-like collar. Just as she wore this style every

day of her adult life, so she wore her hair in the same stiff
little black bob. You don't often see someone with a sewing
basket in a pub, checking coats and hats, contented if
disconnected from the business of the place. My mother
was already bidding goodbye to life and she still loved
Jacqueline Kennedy. The fabric was apple green. In a matter
of weeks I would lean down and kiss her moist refrigerated
head where a tear shone in the corner of one eye, before
she was shoved into the fire, dressed in this very same dress.
I like to believe that it was my vulnerability during the time
of her illness that catapulted me towards McCool. But such
logic isn't natural to me. In any case he leaned on the
counter where I was hidden among wet coats and stared
into my eyes with an expression of astonishment and lust.
"You look like your father," he said, "an Irishman, I wager,
from the west. Are you twenty one?" Being naturally quiet,
I only nodded but when I returned his gaze I saw my fate.
Whether it would happen then and there, or years later, I
could read that he was written in. I was revolted. This
revulsion was a form of fear, but it was also a sign that we
would become intimate before too long. Revulsion often
signals the inevitable. It is a kind of symptom of obedience.

McCool was his singing name by which he was commonly
known and I had hated him every time he took up the guitar
and sang, he was so handsome. But the fact that he came
from Ireland where my grandmother lived – that he was
Irish – thrilled me. Now I had an excruciating pain in my
groin where my ovaries were firing off, and I clutched my
guts. I never got what I wanted. We couldn't take our eyes

off each other. To look was to feel. We were, in this one stare, too attuned. If I was witty, snide, fond, full of fear or sadness, he reacted with the right glance, as in sympathetically. As two who had suffered through similar childhoods – fatherless, mad mothers, foster care – the blood of actual Ireland in his body made him seem more tragic than myself. He was like my mother in his frenzied propensities. My pain was mirrored on his face.

"What hurts?"

"My stomach," I told him.

"Mine too. We need children. Let's have them."

"I need a ring."

"Well, all right then, and let's find a priest."

It was this quick and that easy. His poverty and his intoxicated claims to being Irish reminded me of my mother's intelligence staggered by dread and paranoia. But I was really after my father. The inevitability of our marriage came with the force of an accident. All the contingencies slammed us into a bed trying to produce babies, but unable. We tried and tried. Such a failure was like a funnel that drags you whirling towards its smallest point. Because of it, I would afterwards be able to forgive everyone everything.

Just as Languedoc was a sublime intention realized on earth, Lewis remained my courtly love, the one where joy was untroubled by knowledge. McCool was horribly real. Antigone says, "The God of the Dead at least desires equality," and it certainly is the case that all deaths, no matter how little, are lovely levelers of people. But I was a sucker for him because of his diction. The diction of daddy.

3-4

On one of those wintery days Lewis got Mimi out of prison. Not on probation but out scot free. He had friends in legal places, people who owed him favors and he put them all to work for her. Lewis always kept his promises which is why he rarely made them. Mimi had been inside for one year and six months. Her family came to take her home and I didn't see her again; it was one thing after another.

That same week Ruby took all her things out of her room and left my household, saying she wanted to live with Mimi. She said: "At my age you just want to go home. It's basic. I like the way she cooks those eggs." The women in that family were under the sway of the old man who now insisted that they all return to their house in Missouri. He said he had learned enough in Boston. I lost them all as quickly as I had found them. I felt like a monster banned from society and never loved by you, God, who would never reward me for my troubles. No children, no success. Lewis was in Africa when his family decided to start west and he returned only to boss people around, then sweep away again like a US Senator. He was wonderful at teaching me how to trust and love no man, to live without sex or affection except from my poor children. I was grateful for his annihilating insouciance by the time I was forty. Invisibility by then was my favorite thing. The only time I burned was when people noticed I was white and hated me for it, because then it meant I came from somewhere physical in history.

I decided that Ruby never loved me. She moved in with me only out of perversity – to make her brother – Pop the father – mad. His racism reminded her of the way he had always been cruel to her about her plain looks. She nonetheless went to visit him, even when she hated him, and the day I dropped her there – to return for good – I saw him thinner at the door, his pants baggy and his skin grayish in color. He shouted at me: "What have you heard from my son?"

"He's in Jerusalem."

"Well, tell him to leave Jerusalem and help us move out of this hellish city."

"I will. He will."

"As for you, it was you who let this happen to Mimi," he yelled at me. "White people always fail in the end. No moral attention, only self-interest–"

Ruby pushed him out of her way and they went inside with a bang of the door.

Mansions are resting places, like inns, and God has many of them for people to stop in, on their way home. I don't know why I found such a mansion there, outside that door, that afternoon, but I was flooded with the sky and its lack of names.

9-5

The dialectics of the 20th century (determinism versus choice) is as old as the hills. But today I realized that a choice can be wrong. I used to think otherwise. Now I see that choices are so difficult because people know that they can make the wrong ones. But I think that if a choice is made against you – to reject you, your work or your love, for instance – it can't be wrong. It can't be wrong because it would always come to that, anyway. Sooner or later, you would be rejected by that party. And you would suffer throughout the whole process. So in a way determinism happens to you. But choice happens to others.

In the meantime, and in one's innocence, forward motion drags more and more collected material to the surface of your person. In an ideal situation, when the weight is only a mild hindrance, the person examines the dream-stuff and shucks away the pieces that are the heaviest. I think it might be an error to throw away the recollected things that make you suffer and better to convert them into works. By works I mean actions or objects of beauty or functional value. However, you have to believe that there is no unconscious in order to do this. You have to be committed to wakefulness as a continual and total state of being. Between Brahman and consciousness there is no border. Wakefulness like sleep provides a person with a kind of emotional release since you can swim into nonbeing with your eyes wide open. If you stop thinking of your psyche as a bank, containing hidden capital, you can finally begin to spend your time. Siva and Sakti, Arjuna and Krishna, Mary and the Infant Jesus – these are images of the actual and the open-to-all.

"Scoot closer," Ramakrishna said to his faithful followers. He was alert and affectionate. It is important to remain faithful to something – that is, to finish the same thing over and over. Libby and McCool parted without tears like two little friends who are sick of their stuffed animals and are now ready for school. She was worried about her children who were unruly and dirty and she turned her full attention on them while she lived with a bunch of rich friends in Hawaii. There she was loved and safe. After McCool handed me the deed to the land on the Mexican border, he drove me and the children east, and stalked us for several years. What was his problem? He was convinced that Lewis was sneaking in to see me.

Suspicion is a magician, making fantasies become real.

Lewis did sneak in one night, arriving at my bedside uninvited, drunk. Everyone in the big wooden house was sleeping. There was an autumn wind scratching at pavements and windows and walls. The stairs creaked with nobody on them. The door swung lonely on its hinges. The glass panes banged. Lewis was dressed in a three quarter length black leather coat, wore a black beret and a light beard.

"How did you get in?" I cried.
"The window slid right up."
"Why? Your voice is slurring, you might get caught."
"By who? You're the only authority figure here."

"You know."

"O'Cool is a fraud, a coward, he will never lay a hand on me."

"So why are you here?"

"Pop wouldn't let me in. He's gone crazy."

"Well, am I the only one left?"

"Seems that way. Let me in."

"My bed?"

"Come on, don't worry."

Lewis dropped his coat shoes pants and sweater on the floor and slid in his boxers and tee shirt onto and then into the bed. We scrutinized each other in the light coming from the nodding streetlights outside. He smelled like a gingerbread man, smiled, his eyes heavy. Go to sleep, I told him, and don't worry. He turned on his side facing me and shut his eyes so I could watch his face close up in repose. The nostrils shaped like teardrops, the nose itself small, round and firm, the ears like pink shells pressed against his head, his nappy hair cut close, his wide smooth mouth with crescent lines engraved about a quarter-inch from each corner, no other lines anywhere, his eyebrows light but a furrow just beginning to form almost like a new small delicate bone, his muscular neck disappearing into his shirt where he snored.

I slipped gingerly into the orange aura that wrapped him like swaddling and lay wide awake there. I was wearing a plaid flannel nightgown and he lay his sleeping hand on my hipbone. When I breathed, he snorted and flopped on his other side so now I had his back in my face. And this way I ruminated about sex and remembered it as something that must have been courageous to do. If all exercise requires a dash of courage, sex does especially.

There is no deliverance like no delivery. He had laid down his life beside mine at last.

This is not directly a story about maternalism, about the hours and years of care-taking, rushing to and from pick-ups and drop-offs, the homework, the dressing, the health care, the nursing, cleaning diapers, toilet training, teaching to walk, chasing, fearing, reading, rocking, singing, raging, begging, trudging, lugging, dressing, shoes, clothes, mending and finding, trips to the park and zoos and pushing swings and grocery shopping, comforting and punishing, allowing and bitching, the meals after meals after meals and washings-up and washings-down, broken equipment, lost bottles, toys to be fixed and dresses sewed, the comforting, drying and cleaning, the preaching, forgetting and ironing.

This fake mother was as much mother as motel and as much convent as commune.

Saint Teresa said that ministry and suffering were insepa-rable. She believed that contemplation involved the love of one's neighbor, detachment and humility — these being the three virtues of maternalism as well. She hated dour-faced nuns, those who looked at the faults of others and never at their own. On Trinity Sunday, June 2, 1577 she began to wrote The Interior Castle. The soul she says is like a transparent diamond. It is so beautiful and glittery that it can blind a person approaching it, and make her stop outside. It is blind itself. Entering the soul hurts because it doesn't know how magnificent it is or how it magnifies the face of its servant. Knowledge is a function of the working mind but the soul shines despite the body. If it knew how it shone, it might shrivel from shame and let any servant enter easily. Its blind resistance saves it of course from corruption but it makes the entering servant feel barbaric, the way a mother feels when she lets a nurse give her baby its first shot.

Strange to imagine a diamond with airy rooms inside. But there it is. The soul. I think Saint Theresa understood the dilemma of personhood as a problem with physics, each cell refractive and self-contained, the universe stuck in each one in different positions, and the difficulty in examining it from the outside, when the eyes are on the inside of it.

For instance, in the Fifth Dwelling Place, she writes that the soul experiences separation from the body where "its whole intellect wants to understand what it is actually feeling."

Total attention to one thing of beauty puts the rest of the brain to sleep like the whole castle in *Sleeping Beauty*. Seeing is selective blindness because the shock of the beautiful numbs the rest. Teresa says there is a sweet wine near the heart of a person that makes her feel drowsy when she has recollected deeply. It was during my child-rearing years that I drank that wine and my mind passed through the divine mansions resting and realizing.

I had taken five children dutifully through first
communion, confirmation and to Sunday Mass, while I
hung back and watched my revelations. Two of the children
went home to their families, the other three stayed with
me, and still others came and went on a short-term basis.

The place where Lewis found me that night was the above.
Reading and writing manifestoes in my sleep. At five we
whispered while the dawn pinked and tweeted and Lewis
asked: "What happened to Libby? Is she okay?"
"Yes, she's in Hawaii."
"So why is O'Cool so jealous of you if he ran off with your
best friend?"
"McCool's a hypocrite."
"Crazy sounds more like it. Doesn't he hold himself
accountable?"
"He lacks a conscience, a super-ego."
"Did you ever love him?"
"Did you ever love anyone?"

He didn't answer but lay silent, breathing heavily. So now I
could doze. He was awake and still and the light was up and
Saturday had descended from the sky preserving many from
a day of labor or school. My situation took form as a dream
of leaves and loam and growing things. Movements of snake
and roach and rooms that had branches in them and grass
where there used to be rug. No clothes, no chairs, no people,
but tables and papers and reels of film hanging on clothes-

WISHING AROUND THE EDGES

liner blowing with the twigs and their shadows indoors.
This was no home, more like a rayogram by Man Ray.
God led me into the arcade, an energy sepulcher, the station
where you travel to the other world. Of course it was very
dark with intervals of lights engraved in arcs across the
black air. I was scared knowing I had no will left for myself,
had become like a calf who can't decide when or how
anything will happen. All my life people had referred to
this condition as "obedience" or Zen. But I felt no virtue in
standing abandoned at a black wall. If I was as lively as a
spider, it was only my nerves, but probably I was more like
a piece of flesh on a production line waiting for the plant
to turn on and me to be rolled to dust.

Downstairs four large children were watching cartoons as
Lewis and I stirred in my bed. His hand lay on my head
without weight.

"I could never sleep with you because you're the last stop,
he said gruffly."
"Stop? Thanks, me?"
"Yes, it would be the end of our friendship. The end of me
having fun. I couldn't stand it. I seem to like women I don't
love."
"Yawn. That's the oldest boring story."
"I mean, I have wanted to have sex with you but, you know,
it would have been too demanding. Somehow."
"You, how."
"I would have to end up with you. That would be like dying
young."

"Great."

"It's awful, I mean being one of those pathetic people who always think someone better is coming around the corner. In the end, it's me nobody loves. It's me."

"Your mother did."

"And you. A long time ago."

"You're like someone who sleeps with their hat on."

"Too talkative?"

He pulled up his tee shirt to show me his rounded midriff and slapped it with disgust, saying he was getting fat like his father. I asked: "Could you ever marry a white woman?"

"Probably not, seeing as it would damage my image, whatever that is. We could sneak around. I do that all the time. Anyway you'll never get a man again, with that husband crawling around in the bushes, foster kids, no money, over forty."

We dropped into a silence that was moist. I was hurt, even though I knew I could have stuck my hand down under the covers and inside his boxers and rolled against him. Could have excited him and held him and his lingam and played with it until he was locked into the act, both of us smiling and pretending we were smiling. I could have seen it through like a tank entering a forest. We could have done a lot without even being intimate, our eyes shut, diamonds on our inner lids, and roaring brains shutting off the clamor of cartoons. Once Libby told me that one tantra divides the vulva into ten parts that are made for each aspect of the

Great Mother. All tantras have at their center five sacraments:
wine, fish, meat, grain and sex. Every act is holy because
every act is holy. Tantric sex should take place among
flowers, incense, colorful rice, sandalwood, a vessel full of
native rum, sweetmeats and little cakes, but it hardly ever
does. The lotus and the color red are reminders of happy
and mystical sex. On the slopes of some blue mountain
there is a yoni-shaped hole in a rock and it weeps red tears
and water that makes you high. Someone said that a drop
of Christ's red blood contains the universe. For the rest of
us, it is just the cells in our skins and brains. Later we ate
fruit loops and drank orange juice in front of the t.v. with
Ruby and the kids and then Lewis went away to South Africa
and his fateful encounter with a gun.

While Lewis was gone I met a sailor who had tattoos on his
arms, as blue as his eyes, a reddish mustache and a veiny
face from drink. He was introduced as McCool's revolutionary cell mate and a sailor who had crossed the seven
seas on rigs and tankers. He was funny and quiet and
meticulous. When he stayed with us, he was always straight-
ening and lining up the children's toys and stuffed animals,
and placing them in interesting relations to each other, ones
that the children shrieked with laughter over, when they
came home. He cleaned and tidied my cupboards too, and
swabbed out the grimy drawer where the flatware lay in
rubbermaid containers.

He stayed in my house while McCool was playing music
somewhere south. The sailor drank rum in his juice in the

morning, his face fired up and he told me jokes.

Over the afternoons when the children were still in school and I was home from work, we'd sit in the kitchen with tea and chocolate chip cookies that I was baking, and he would arrange everything in sight. One night he got into my bed and made love to me. He was strong, his hands slow, his approach tender but unremitting. He was making me laugh all the time. We had beside the bed rum, candies, a candle, incense and red rosary beads from India. The laughter lasted all night, then at daybreak he snuck back to his room and snored loudly, leaving that afternoon. On his way out he told me my husband was a pathological liar and not Irish at all.

"We met on the merchant marine near Indonesia," he said. "I hate to be the one to break it to you, but you ought to know the facts." He was a plain ruddy man, nothing to look at, and I thought at first he was joking. After all his jokes occurred in direct ratio to his withheld violence. A roar of laughter replaced gunfire. But this time he didn't smile. And I felt like a thorny tree that cannot spout a bud at its head, a long stiff stem with its conclusion in air. "You mean – his accent – is a fake?" He nodded and I thanked him as he went out the door, while the children pulled on his sleeves, begged him to stay and called him Popeye.

It struck me as a familiar experience that shock could be administered not in a cold voice but through a mist of hugs and kisses. I had been wooed by a forgery.

9–6

Libby flew me and my children to Hawaii one year. She paid for everything. We took three different planes, the last being a miniature one out of Honolulu into Hilo. It was raining where she lived in a wooden house beside a waterfall. Geckos climbed the walls. Six people lived with her in the house, two of them being her children, and they all had expensive four-wheel-drive cars. One was a man as thick as a heifer who acted like Zeus. His girlfriend was the school friend named Honey. Then Libby's lover had slicked back hair and strong features that found their focus in his bad teeth. He looked as if he had dirt in his bones. He had been a maker of documentaries, got into drugs, joined the religious group, gave up drugs and was now selling real estate in Kona. The hour I arrived, I was spirited away by Libby who never liked me near her real friends. She had rented a house on black sand for us all and there we stayed with our children. Was she ashamed of me? Or was she proud and wanted me to herself? She told me how she left her purse open for those men in the past, and they took her money freely and spent it on drugs and housing. We tripped along the dark sea's edge with our children and wished we were lesbians. Libby also wished she was somewhere else, she always did, wanting to be in New York when she was in New Mexico or wanting to be California when she was in Hawaii, she believed she was missing something important.

I told her I hadn't yet used the deed to her property on the border and she assured me that she really wanted me to go and fix it all up because then we could hide away together there, when the time came, when the Millennium and the Apocalypse came, and when we were very old. "It should be a force for good. McCool was at his best there, and so was I."

"What is real sex?" I asked her.

"Lying in bed with the one you love, or screwing a stranger?"

"That's like asking what is the difference between celibacy and chastity."

"There is a difference."

"What."

"Celibacy is the choice to be single, unsexual. Chastity is something you don't choose, it's a condition – of incorruptibility. You can be raped and still be chaste."

"Which would you rather be?" Libby asked me. We squinted across black twinkly sand to a sea so bright, it rejected eyesight. "I'd rather the one that isn't a choice," I told her.

THE GLASS THAT GREW

10-1

Three days a week I worked in a darkroom editing film, then video, then learning how to correlate images with monitors, and how to use an elaborate toaster for after-effects and then having to learn digital editing. The company was financially solvent, run by a practical idealist named Rye who believed in the power of the media to change public opinion for the good. He was a perpetual Pan and a Catholic convert. Later he moved to Honduras to educate people in technology. For the years I worked for him I was happy in the dark. At home Ruby was there for the kids, along with others who came, stayed and went away. Ruby, disabled in an accident when she fell down an elevator shaft at a poorly run charcoal briquet factory, moved stiffly giving orders. She was by nature tyrannical. Like Lewis her nephew. Some perverse streak in her resisted accomplishment and sought salvation in struggling with objects and other people's needs. She was a Catholic who did everything "for God" when she could have worked in a powerful secular organization as an executive producer. Rewards, flattery and any other form of attention sickened her. Yet she suffered when she was ignored and wanted to make sure she was appreciated. She was always mad at Lewis and she only saw us together once, that morning in front of television after nothing happened.

My feelings for her went, "Help, Mommy, don't leave me, please love me. I hate everyone and everyone hates me. But not you, please not you!"

Outside our house two tall swaying phone poles, pines and stone, cars nearly crashing at the intersection every fifteen minutes, and a stinkweed tree.

10-2

Tom and I leave our compound and drive to the desert the day the rain retreats and the day after the doctor's visit. We have decided to look for the center for abused children, just to see. You climb up to get down in this desert. You drive about 4000 feet above sea level on winding roads through monumental bodies of green-hard hills, buzzed with bracken and mustard and tearing up any shadows. Unusable glens and pastures all dry. Five black bears and a jaguar had been spotted by residents recently.

Campers have seen coyotes, gophers, lizards and snakes. California oak trees remind Tom of paintings by Corot and Millet. He feels as if he has exploded into one of their canvases when we drive through a thicket and a tunnel of these dotty oaks, because when we walk on them the leaves are tough curls that crackle underfoot like hardened oil paint. I don't know why the mountains look as if they are bent backs moving forward as we approach them. We are speechless for a half hour at being far from our grievous hideaway and the tropical drops of the canyons and the dripping trees. It is mid-February. It is Valentine's Day.

He tells me that Jesus thought of the heart as an organ of intellect and quoted: "Out of the hearts of men proceed evil thoughts."

"It sounds to me as if Jesus means that emotions precede ideas."

"We're dropping into the desert now."

"Did we bring that water?"

This desert begins as a pallid field speckled with round cactus, then some crown of thorns loop up and over, the ground beachy and shelly, quartz and granite bits embedded in the brokenness like dusty trash-heaps from the 19th century. Heaps not hills and down we roll onto the flat plain, almost badlands, dry-dry and dappled with a variety of cactus red-tipped yellow-tipped or flat purple spatulas dimpling thorns. Still, the light of it all is blinding. I press at my eyes, try to shield them, squint, blink and water. My friend is dazzled in other ways. As we drive towards a little town corrupted by a country club, he confesses to liking a sense of anarchy that the desert gives off. It reminds him of Mary of Egypt who walked stark naked across the sand with only her hair to cover her, aroused by visions and penances.

"And who does Mary of Egypt remind you of?" I ask him and my tongue feels like my heart because I am scared of his feelings for people.

"No one. Why? Who?"

"Maybe Gemma?"

"Well, I guess," he surmised.

"Do you think you can, um, enter a monastery with this kind of interest?"

"What interest."

"I mean, can you live a celibate life?"

"Well, that's the point."

"Of?"

"Of all this."

"You mean, to learn to hate everything?"

"Not everything." He waved his hand vaguely towards the cloud-free sky.

"Not Gemma?"

"Not everything in the world," he said with a glowering glance at me.

"Well, anyway," I said. "I can't think symbolically."

"But you do all the time. Thought is symbolic. Language is too."

"Then I mean something else."

"Mythologically, mythically, maybe," he patiently suggested.

"Well, I can't think of an idea outside of experience."

"Thinking with your heart?"

"I'm a mother type."

"Ma they called you? Your foster kids?"

"Each one called me something different. Ma, Mummy, Mom. Henny."

"Well, I'm not called Dad, Daddy, Papa or Father, and never will be."

"You chose this," I tell him.

"Of course, I know, but I mean, Gemma's child, I love him."

"It would be hard not to."

"Won't you take care of him? He needs a home. His foster parents are not good."

"I know about foster parenting first hand," I remind him.

THE GLASS THAT GREW

"See? It's all intended," he said.

"Don't you want to ask what was wrong? Why I couldn't have children? If I minded?" I wonder, then say, "Forget it."

"I just feel that it's intended, that you are meant to be his parent, because of the Julio connection, I guess, and well, other reasons too."

"You feel guilty about Gemma. But are you in love with her?"

"God no."

"I thought there had been someone–maybe her–"

"God no."

"Who then who."

"Forget it. It's another story."

It is impossible for me to ask the inevitable question: Are you gay? The image of Mimi's closet is not far off. Denial, embarrassment, not wanting to know, because it will so profoundly exclude me from the history of his future.

I squint now at the horizon where there is a metallic glitter poured across the dust. Huge khaki colored war planes are hunched on a vast spread of land, behind high fencing. We slow to look, from our closed car, now outside the town.

"You seem upset," he says to me.

"I am but I don't know why."

"Those planes."

"No, I was before."

"I think I know why," he says.

"Why."

"You don't like thinking I have – had – ordinary feelings."

"I do like it."

"No, all of you lay people hate it. It makes you anxious, and angry at me. You would rather imagine me as uncontaminated, pure, innocent, whatnot."

"I do like thinking that one person I know lived without violence," I admit.

"It's bigger than that," Tom says. "It's existential. It's a wish for God to be here, on earth, visible."

The war planes seem abandoned. The site they occupy is absolutely without a sign of human life. But the sound of one buzzing in the faraway cut the air like the shape of a dog. "Don't worry. I won't tell you anything personal," Tom says and speeds up the car. "Give me that water."

Soon we pull into a diner called Hart's Chicken Parts which is also deserted except for one red-cheeked waitress watching television. She brings us sandy-like slices of chicken and cole slaw and Coke. "Eckhart talks about the birth of God out of nothingness," Tom says with his napkin covering his mouth, "and the nothingness is swollen like a pregnant woman. That's the image he uses."

"I wonder why," I murmur.

"And so it's sort of like the universe as physicists describe it now."

"It is? I wish we were outdoors again."

"Why did you marry your husband?"

"I think, I guess, we had something awful in common. Class anxiety. We were both outsiders. Libby was our shared object of adoration. God, analysis is boring."

"You women just after the Beats! My generation and class? Your age group too? Well, you got an awful batch of men," said Tom. Bastards. Still believed they were demi-gods, spoiled, but angry when you began to get independent. Awful. I feel for you. You got a raw deal. The new generation of boys is better. So why didn't you have children?"

"Let's go outside. Him. He couldn't. Weak sperm or something."

Through the plate glass window and across the black stripe of highway, the ground was all white now, and hard to locate. "You could have left him," said Tom. "I mean, that's a legitimate reason to."

"Tom, are you sure that boy is not your child?"

"I swear. Julio Solito, gone far east, is the father. He hates America.'

"Does he even know he has this child?"

"No."

10-3

It is snowing and I am watching from the window as the ground silvers. The brick around me is almost uniformly dark except in three other windows three other solitary women are staring out towards the river that is screened by a curtain of snowdrops. Mimi in her cell complained of one thing only, and that was the difficulty of finding anything beautiful to look at. She told me that she had a magnifying glass, just a little round solid stone sized cheap thing, and she would turn it around and around in a shaft of light in order to be mesmerized by the multiple whirls it concocted across objects. "Dreams describe the world as it feels." I hear the bumping and wonder what it sounds like in the apartment below. Sex probably. Or someone building a city in a closet.

A movie moves in place like certain minds when they think of a piece of river. They gave me a dark cone that night in time, me alone on an institution lawn and lots of night poured from that vessel scarred by twinklers (only the ones I couldn't see). I asked a woman for a ride back to my place, she wasn't very nice but said yes. Then all the lights were out everywhere and I thought of sleeping on the little balcony but it might break and fall into all those citizens whispering out there. Then they sent me my guard and he was checking his arms in a thin-lipped red-cheeked jovial Nazi way. His arms were okay so he left for his own place somewhere in the dark. I called this film *"Magnificat"*.

Once, during an all-night vigil in 902 AD, at a church in Constantinople, Andrew, a holy fool and his friend Epiphanios, saw the Mother of God. She was high above them in the air, surrounded by saints. Her veil was like a vessel painted with sails that whirled out for miles protecting people who didn't want to die at sea. I bet her veil was dark blue and spangled with sequins and blinding.

Now I am being easily enchanted which makes me worry that I will not have the courage to go through with my plan. The falling snow across my line of vision is equivalent to

music entering my ears. That is, it gives me the impression
that I am only a machine built to observe it. I *am nothing*
would be written on my ceiling soon, slashes of shadow
from moving cars outside.

One by one the other women turn away, draw the shades,
disappear. There is no bumping now and the boy is sleeping.

The camera stays turned on the water but only snow blown
on air is shown. My mother returned conciliatory from my
film her grave which was really her genre. She was young
and kind walking with me to work through this snow.

I dared to say things. We were in Dublin and she replied as
you would hope anyone would, with civility, affection,
appreciation and concern because I had forgotten my lunch.
I don't know where we were or where that park was
situated or what city is both medieval and gray and also a
seaside resort. That's why I chose Dublin. But maybe it was
a city in the next generation, a purgatorial condo settle-
ment on the way around, where the dead congregate in
their best suits and spirits for the difficult treck towards
annihilation. She was so motherly, it nearly killed me – she
was all that I ever wanted! She said we have plenty of time.
Let's go back home and get it. The sky was dawning inkily,
clouds unzipping and letting out some blue and yellow
puffs. It was cold in that snow but my mother encrypted in
her dream being was good-natured about it even when she
erred, and we turned the wrong way through the years, the
hulls of the buildings as close as young breasts.

I wanted to save my mother's history from the eye of the holy spirit so I aspirated and dispirated, trying to fog up the air around her with my own breath. When in *The Stranger* Merseault's mother died, he was finally open to the "benign indifference of the universe." That's why I called that one *Mother Hen*.

10-4

"One day, as a young magpie flew over the meadow, something cold and white fell in her eye. Then it fell again and again. She felt as if a little veil were drawn across her eyes while the small, pale, blinding white flakes danced around her. The magpie hesitated in her flight, fluttered a little, and then soared straight up into the air. In vain. The cold white flakes were everywhere and got into her eyes again. She kept flying straight up, soaring higher." "Don't put yourself out so much, dearie," a crow who was flying above her in the same direction called down, "don't put yourself out so much. You can't fly high enough to get outside these flakes. This is snow."

Henny's mother liked to quote that crow in *Bambi*. "Don't put yourself out," she would say to her daughter loudly.

This practice had to do with her own breakdown and wanting her daughter to believe that she might die in a fire like Bambi's mother. She wanted this child to save her from despair and watched her with dog-like desire ("Is she putting on her shoes to take me for a walk!") and twisted her fingers together excitedly. Her daughter was unhappy with her, and unhappy leaving her because of her failure to provide her mother with her deepest satisfaction which might be death. In fact the mother got impatient with her daughter when she studied and did homework and wanted her to pay attention to her, so she chatted and taught her to cook and sew instead of study. Her mother had a brain that was deluged like sea-sponge in salty emotional waves. She talked about her own dying hopefully and hoarded belladonna in case she wanted to kill herself one day. Her daughter wanted to be the one to kill her if she needed it and the one to rescue her if she changed her mind. This was because she loved her mother or was attached to her; pitied her; and longed for her to say in a sane voice that she was the most wonderful child in the whole world.

When they were on good terms, her mother read to herself only – Dickens, Hardy, the Russians, the Brontes – and let her read quietly herself. Her mother once had a dream that she was Anne Bronte raised to the same status as her sisters. She was in love with Bramwell and the father whom she said was "quite a sexpot," being Irish and shooting his gun off at the parsonage walls.

Henny's mother loved Libby and so she prophesied the worst for her. And considering she was a maid, Libby thought her mother was pretty smart and intuitive. But Libby was sometimes ashamed of being friends with a maid's daughter and cultivated other friendships at the

Mystic school, ones among girls who were glamorous like Honey Figgis or brilliant and tragic like a schoolmate named Mary who disappeared.

Still, the two of them studied ventriloquism together and threw their voices through clenched teeth in front of any number of strangers. Libby continued to practice ventriloquism all her life, in her car or bathroom, when she was alone. It was a deflection of solitude and was related to her obsessive face-making. In New York in the late sixties and early seventies she was admired by a variety of intellectual and artistic men, despite her Charlie McCarthyisms. She was filmed and painted. She go-go danced on the stage in the East Village, was photographed in the nude and voted Slum Goddess of the East Village. She was skinny, drug-addicted, terrified, but never without dignity. Like a disciplined dancer who gets drunk, or an animal in a crowd of violent humans, she stood out as being complete. Still, she was dubbed The Broken Arrow by someone famous.

"Higher than that unmanifest state, there is another unmanifested eternal being who does not perish when all beings perish. This unmanifested (state) is called the Indestructible. They call that the highest goal from which, having been obtained, beings don't return."

It was the expression on the face of a fetus she aborted several weeks into her pregnancy that caused the moment of conversion for her. "Find yourself if you're going to lose me!" its face squeezed out to her.

"Once you become aware of yourself as seeker, you are lost," Thomas Merton wrote. Now the woodland in her was green and bending when she escaped for Big Sur. While Edie Sedgwick and her beautiful dark brothers Bobby and Minty with their warm full mouths and eyes would perish, Libby struggled to outlive that era. She had to leave behind the brown lines of Central Park, leaf-settled and wintery under the stones, in order to become disciplined.

So for years she was gone from me. While I sank a decade deep away from my former friends and acquaintances, becoming immersed in children and the time they required, McCool danced around the edges of our slum-estate playing tricks on the kids. Streams of bullshit poured from his lips as he swayed on our broken steps forbidden by law to cross the threshold. Whenever he was down and out, he called them for consolation, always asking, "How's Ma?" But since the truth drove him mad, we all got good at lying, displacing the facts by a few inches, writing fiction.

Ramakrishna rolled in the dust crying "Ma! Ma! Ma!" for Kali.

Aurobindo said that wider Hinduism was not limited to India but had lots of scriptures, including the Veda, Vedanta, Gita, Upanishad, Darshana, Purana, Tantra, not to forget the Bible and the Koran.

"However," he continued, "its real, most authoritative

scripture is in the heart in which the Eternal has His dwelling."

"Is there still an above and a below?" asked Nietzsche shocked at finding himself riding on a ball in the sky.

10-5

In the great blizzard, just as it was during the black-out in New York, there was no white and the other black, but behavior. Snow wouldn't stop graying and flying, filling, splitting, spinning, windblown, rising as it fell into itself. I loved my husband three times – once when I saw him giving a homeless man the coat he was wearing through snow.

Once when he almost got off the train too late, after saying goodbye to me and the children and tripped in the gap between the train and the platform. And once when he came out of the clinic knowing that it was his own infertility that was the problem. Sometimes we lay in the dark of our bed holding hands. Sometimes you hear a horse neigh in a movie with one of those painful squeals that old doors get. It can be a man crying. In February, out west, the robin is already fat. There is silver lichen hanging off trees. It reminds me of this snow and not of literature.

"If you'd weave seven locks of my head into the web and fasten it with the pin into the wall, then I'd weaken and be like any man," said Samson to Delilah, but then he was able to do it himself pulling the pin, the loom and the web off the wall. She believed he was belittling her with this trick and so avenged him. Three moments of true love are more like nails than pins. Compassion is the emotional term for that grueling sting.

I am haunting the ghosts. You can after all get sick from a dream. Projectile vomit, or projective verse – they are interchangeable in a dream. In a nightmare you can develop the germ for your own death. You can cultivate it in your heart. Once I walked towards my mother's apartment, wearing her hat, and longing to lie on the sofa there beside her, while she said, "Rest, dear, rest." But then Mimi hurled herself over the hood of her Ford, climbed around inside looking for dirty laundry that had spilled, angrily sobbing Can't you help? to Lewis in the backseat beside his wheelchair. Because she felt so sorry for him.

Lewis told me this: "I was sent out with a bunch of foreign journalists across these ice-cracked fields. To follow families being chased from one country into another, where they were supposed to be kept in refugee camps. There were about three hundred of them, moving in rough formation, rag tag as they say. Rag tag. December bedouins. Our van stopped at the crest of a field striped brown, shining with patches of ice still. We saw troops coming towards the people, about a quarter mile away, and watched them gather, climbing out of their trucks, around the people. Men were being pulled from their screaming families and made to kneel, the way you always see it in the movies, hands behind head, and then there was shooting and all the bodies folded into their blood. I mean folded. We didn't know what to do, weirdly, we sat there, paralysed, paralysed, while a couple of the trucks drove up to where we sat. These burly guys got out and asked who was what. British? German? French? American? Turk? Everyone was nervously telling the truth and pulling out press cards and i.d.'s and I don't know what came over me but I said Catholic, when they asked me, knowing they hated Catholics even more than Jews and Muslims. So then while all the others were fumbling around, smoking, laughing, cracking out jokes, my brain was thinking words to describe what I just saw — carnage, massacre, incident, litter, atrocity — when one of them just shot me, blam, in the side."

10-6

With a miniature image of the beloved implanted in me, I think my body is both a garden and a factory. A habitat that is a factory. A factory empty of electricity, but a little productive. About like a desert which is no place for a couple. There the sage smells like silver at a table set for animals.

To tell someone that a person contains the blueprint of the cosmos can be misleading because the person can't just lean over and read it. The blueprint doesn't exist without someone beaming the light on it and I hate to say it, but this operation takes a lifetime of excruciating searching. I can't say that the description of this blueprint forms "another" level of reality because I would automatically be separating them with the word "another".

I am in this one making dough figures who exist in a state of attention. They are waiting to be eaten. This is not "another" way of describing what happened, as if what happened was a thick and settled thing – like a castle that one could stand and contemplate. Objects rest from their flight only when you look at them without seeing them. I was so invisible, even birds rested mid-flight when my camera arrived because they didn't sense my presence at all.

It is important not to pin ideas down because they can turn into false gods. "To let the real God remain free and clear sometimes requires atheism," Lewis said once. I don't remember what he was wearing on that given day so the words have to stand in for the details.

"The church is a boat so well built that it lets you sail into the horrifying darkness and mystery and allows you to drift, to explore, because it is fit for wind and stars, over centuries constructed to meet unexpected squalls and drops. It doesn't eliminate the horror or the mystery, it just helps you enter them…." Tom tells his hands that are pulling at stones.

I would like to tell him that God has already crushed me into powder. Holy-talk has begun to calcify and bone into that powder too. Those refugees on the road, whose children, wives and husbands and friends were executed, know what it is to be left languishing in time. You can be buried alive in blue air and still walk around in a soft coat of gold. But will there be less of God or of me after It has pressed out its energy here? Will It expend Itself? The word holy needs to be eliminated. The Emperor Wu wondered how the word void could be used when everything is void. But "died" is even stranger than "void" because to have "died" is to no longer exist, so there can't be any word for it. At least, however, it is in the past tense. I don't like the word "worship" either, God, because it is idolatrous to separate yourself from God like that.

The divine wafer is baked light as is the cremated body. Swallow the sticky circle it is paste and reduces to the size of an orange seed and goes down with only a little residue stuck in the mouth. Saint Ignatius built a palace full of little rooms for each memory. He could this way wander in and out at will. To let the memories disperse and vaporize all over the mansion would be to lose them as the sleeping shepherd loses the sheep.

It is like the shape of a tall brooding mountain smeared with shadow and black bracken and how it seems to be the last shape the dream might build before it is covered by sun.

Until you see the desert behind the mountain what should be a luscious field is now a pile of bleached bones. The color of the desert is bone. It crumbles, scratches underfoot just like this snowy New England street. Not to become hard or cold is my goal.

We walked on snow leaving the car shining behind us and I was moved somehow to tell what I had done. "Now will you do me a favor?" I asked him… I hated his lack of response when he stopped walking and I crunched on alone into the white. The snow stops very suddenly as in all at once after midnight. Snow, which cooperates only with itself, is caused as if by consensus. The sky clears away clouds and lays open its sparking dogstars. The color of the ground is diluted ink, the river thick and iced. Only one light in the building is turned on and hidden behind a shade. As long as the desire to do something is in me, it is not time to do it.

In the third dynasty of Ur, in Sumer, three thousand years before Christ, a dreambook described a woman holding a gold stylus and studying a cold slab of stone on which the stars in the heavens were perfectly inscribed. She was Nidaba the goddess of writing. In fact, she was in this image a kind of architect advising people to build their temples according to the outlines of the heavens. She also says to me: Write in stone!

"Did you perhaps love your husband?" Tom asks.
"What do you mean?"
"Well, why didn't you leave him? Why are you protecting him?"
"Me? From what?"
A veridical dream is the 46th part of prophecy.

NONE CAN GO BEYOND

11.1

Lizards, two at once, speed past my feet to another shadow.

Tamar's father-in-law Judah met her in the desert and thought she was a prostitute, because she wore a veil in order to blind him from her true identity. He slept with her by the side of the road and obligingly gave her his seal, his cord and his staff as evidence that it was he who had screwed her. When she gave birth to twins, a scarlet thread was tied onto the hand of the first one out, but he withdrew his hand, back into the womb, and out came the second baby first. Birthrights and entitlements, since the beginning of recorded time, have been evidence of pride as the first human error. People dread equality. They want to establish disparity more than anything else.

First, they wondered, which child was the firstborn. Then: why had this woman been so determined to reinvigorate her husband that she slept with his father?

If scientists could revive the eggs or semen of the dead, then that would be something far sweeter than cloning. The desert produces a variety of tough sticky plants that you can cook and eat, and some sage and threadlike red flowers. All of these seem however to be leftovers rather than the foundation of new life on earth. The ghost of ocean hangs over them, days of wetness and supplement.

When I climb to the crest of the bony hill and see official

buildings out on the flatland beyond, wires sparkling like a Christmas car antenna, and the usual configuration of drab clay-toned buildings with a panopticon at the center, I turn to call Tom to come and see. He is looking at something else in the other direction.

In the next twenty years surely that center for abused children will be replicated from coast to coast in the form of a prison, each one asking "What is the relationship of crime to crime?"

"I know," Tom says. "It's a gloomy prospect."
"Shall we go down, closer, visit?" Not even the Sabbath exists in such transparency.

"When the embodied one is about to leave the body, When he frees himself from it, what is left here? That, just that! That is the Pure, that is Brahman, that is called The Immortal; in him all the worlds are established and none can go beyond."

"No," he says. "Let's not."

11-2

"Why have you rejected me, bitch?" McCool kept asking me. "Why have you thrown me out of my own home? I admit that I did wrong, but now I want to come home! You should see where I sleep. I want to be back with the children. I will be good and babysit, just let me come back."

He appeared at the door banging, shouting and had to be led away by police or friends. When he was raving like that, he always threatened Lewis whom he had never met. Racial skirmishes and marital squabbles crossed paths, the courts being packed with abuse cases, many of them dropped in the courtroom on the way to the bench, the women too afraid of the men to testify. McCool arrived drunk at his custody hearing which didn't help his case. The times he saw the children he was often drunk too, and playing in a pub, while a woman took care of them. He played traditional Celtic tunes alone and with others, and the children were proud of him like that. Once I saw him at a distance and didn't know it was him, and thought, that's a handsome man. He was walking along Centre Street with a woman behind carrying a guitar in a black case. She was talking animatedly to some other woman, I was in my car, and when I realized it was him, the children did too and called his name. He called back to them excitedly and said, Hi, Ma, as if he was one of them, but that wasn't one of the times that I loved him. Shouts, waves, recognition, scattering the bitter losses.

11-3

During the Reagan years, Libby returned, desperate, needing a place for herself and her children to stay, when she got the idea of going back to school to become an expert in health care. But it took her several years before the idea took form. This was when she also had the thought that she had to radically change her life in order to save herself and her children. Even while she dragged on pot, she remembered when it was time to meditate, because she had returned from her training in California. "I only get shocked by how big the universe is," she said, "when I am feeling big myself.... When I am feeling small, the universe seems tiny too. Because I can carry it around with me, even in the dark. Do you know what I mean, Hen?"

This is also the time when she saw my husband building a shed outside and asked me to tell her more about him, and soon they were having an affair. I was laughing over garlic. My nails were black from the winter-hard garden. Bulbs had been buried that morning, and I was strangely glad when I saw her slip out and embrace him hello and his look of wonder.

How could the dead return to you except through sleep. All encounters in dreams are indications that relationships travel without their people. In those days before holy-talk, but when I had many insights, I only inclined towards aridity in my spirit but my body's storms would not leave me alone. Moods and longings besieged my walls. Working in the dark with cameras, monitors and knobs and watching the images for mergers in design and color, spotting sudden moving gestures from the ghosts on screen, I was a sucker for film but at the mercy of my body. It suffered me while it struggled for a second of peace. Was a woman built to be solitary, thoughtful, maternal, hard-working, hateful and God-crazy all at the same time?

"Why don't you love him?" Libby asked me.

NONE CAN GO BEYOND

"I don't know."

"It's the Lewis obsession. You have got to forget Lewis and appreciate what you have."

She was blindly looking inside herself alone while I gazed out the window at McCool joking on the corner. He might have been a phenomenon the Indians call a Kesi, he looked so wild that day.

There is no world in which a Kesi belongs – free as the wind, thrilled beyond all feeling common to others, intoxicated like a beggar or a maniac; in India the Kesi supports himself on his own spirit. Solitude and silence, total nudity, no memory, no sign, drunk. He is, to some, a sage. Mother is one of his names.

"Ma! Mom! Mommy! Ma!" the children that day squawked around me and Libby, each one with a separate demand.

"I have to help you get free," said Libby. "You've become nothing but a mother to other people's children!"

Actually she and I were ignoring our children and watching McCool on the windowglass, where he was imprinted and sliding around like something pressed there.

He was tearing off his winter jacket and wrapping it over the shoulders of a hunched homeless man with a big chin. "He looks like Edy's father in *On the Waterfront*, that man," I said to Libby.

"What's McCool doing to him?"

"It looks like he's giving him his coat."

"To keep? Maybe he doesn't want it?"

The old man struggled to get his arms in the over-large sleeves while McCool jiggled the jacket around from behind, unconscious of our witnessing.

"Yes," I said. "He wants it. I mean, McCool does. But."

"That's so nice of him," Libby whispered reverently. McCool, arms akimbo, shivered and stamped like a horse.

11-4

You have to live a ridiculous life in the eyes of America in order to make a livelihood for five on part-time poorly paid work. Renting out rooms helped, so that the house from top to bottom was filled with people, the kitchen available to all of them. The house had mattresses scattered throughout and plastic boxes for clothes, books and toys. It was an odd habitat, a noisy place where conversions took place before even the revolutionaries knew it. My tenants included an enlightened idiot, a pauper, a poor villager, a former cow-keeper, a current bookkeeper, and a scholar.

For many years Lewis and I talked heatedly without a third person to tell us the secret of our relationship. But the meaning of such things is revealed only when both parties are separated and have no hope of seeing each other again. After our first meeting, when we were that young, he and I kept meeting accidentally. This went on for years. He behaved like one guarding the seen from the unseen. He never wanted me to know what he was really doing but invented stories about his private life and laughed at my belief. He jumped around excitedly, his brow furrowed and a smile at the clouds. Sometimes he took me into a coffee shop to show me what he was studying.

He was twenty five when he read this: "Within the sphere of circulation capital passes through the two antithetical phases C-M and M-C; it is immaterial in which order... Commodities to money and money to commodities. We are concerned here with only the general character of the costs of circulation which arise out of the metamorphosis of forms alone."

"I am a Marxist," he said.

"It is just as if somebody," wrote St. John of the Cross, "were to see something he has never seen before and the like of which he has never seen... Despite all efforts he would not be able to give it a name nor to say what it is, even though he perceived it with his senses. How much less will he then be able to speak about a thing he has not received with his senses?"

"I thought you were a Catholic," I said.
"They are compatible," Lewis assured me.

He was feeling cocky and youthful the day he volunteered to go out in that van with the other journalists. He had seduced a beautiful Lebanese woman the night before, and the other American journalist was sick, so he said he would go in his place. He was in his thirties.

Mimi cried and screamed in her Ford and they flew her to him in a hospital in Rome where he was given his first wheelchair and taught how to lift his lower torso from chair to bed to toilet to table. Mimi stayed with him until he could come home. All these spaces but no structures suggest an adaptation to promise. Or a preference for waiting. Or maybe a gift for lacking. His body grew bigger from sitting and more bitter. Jefferson said that people perish when there is no vision guiding them. Lewis said he could tell that everyone wanted to know if he could still have an erection. It was all they really wanted to know.

"Should I carry a card reading Still Functional?" he wondered.

"I don't know," I answered.

I wrote him letters everywhere he went though it is hard to remember how I always knew where he was. Once he actually cared, saying, "I was waiting for your letter. Why did you take so long?"

"Sorry. I'm raising several children," I wrote on my postcard back to him.

And I watched every day for the blue uniform slowly meandering between trees and garbage cans to deliver the mail. It always arrived late in the day, just before dark in the winter. Hardly ever did a letter come to me from Lewis though once a box was left on our steps, and I almost threw

It away, it looked like junk. It was a box of dates, with a card reading "eat one for every date we never had."

Our voices became both acrid and tender over the wires. Our laughter lowered. A woman always feels sorrow towards her son. Soon each of us could identify the other by the ring of the phone's bell while in all other ways he lacked psychic abilities.

"It's Lewis," I would know. Would you rather be an angel or a nun? At least an angel can fly, even through the dead zone.

One day Lewis didn't recognize me for the first seconds when he saw me coming. It was definitely me, rounded around. Because my hair was white and my face had softened, he didn't see what he remembered. I was at the age where I felt like a driver who has turned into her car.

"Behold, the lady of the phone calls," he finally said. We went into a bar, he wheeling ahead of me, bald and heavy set. I could see that he would become his father's weight if it weren't for the work required of his upper torso. Swinging as so many children do back and forth in perdition between one parent's indulgence and another's repression, he would never settle between Mimi and Pop. "I'm only working on one issue now," he told me.

"Prisons?" I asked.
"Right. Night and day. Have you ever been inside of one?"

"Doing time or visiting?" I almost shrieked. "You know I have visited your mother a million times. This is me you are talking to."

"Oh right."

"How's Pop?"

"He's fading out. Your husband?"

"He's still haunting even though all foster kids have grown and gone."

"God, you don't do that anymore?"

"I'm now alone."

"Well you did your job for the universe. Let's make a documentary."

"On?"

"Attica etcetera."

"Good title."

"I can get the money but I need an assistant, you."

"I would like to," I told him.

"Saki?" he offered. Soon the alcohol burned down our walls.

"Libby?" he asked. "Where is she?"

"Here, getting a degree in holistic medicine."

"Wow. Is she still beautiful?"

"Yes, no one on earth looks like her."

"That's the thing. That's the thing."

"Her children are doing well. She is devoting herself to them." I told him.

"Does she have a man?"

"No! She swears she is finished with all that."

"Great, great. Sometimes I think I should have married her."

"Because you love her or because she can pass as

Wampanoag?

"I'm not proud of that, but racism is all over the world. I've seen it literally everywhere. So in that sense, racism isn't about so-called race at all."

"So then what is it about?" I asked.

"Racism would not exist if no one could see." His own face blended into the shady contours of the bar while his eyes smiled and shone. "But everyone can."

"Then it's structural. Not everyone," I said.

"Let's talk about the documentary, my dear one."

"Attica?" I asked.

11-5

In a prison waiting room you want to turn everyone into a ghost and slip through the walls all in a line floating out into the atmosphere. "I know. That would be grand," Tom said and folded his arms and turned in on himself as he did whenever he was there. He averted his face from me and Mimi and spoke in low tones to his wild-haired soul-mate in her green uniform. She had one of those beautiful hard-boned faces that grow better with age, the lines grooved to match the best of expressions – laughter and surprise. She could have been Algerian but she was white American. She would never speak to me though she was friends with Mimi.

"How is your prayer life?" I heard her ask him once when I was silent with Mimi. They both cracked up laughing, almost hysterically, bent over, head to head, rocking. I liked to eavesdrop on their conversations but he spoke in such hushed tones I couldn't catch a single word. I liked his misery at being there and the way it came out as hysteria. Between their bodies there was some electrical force that made them each buckle and shriek with laughter. It was out of character. But when she asked how her son had been behaving, the hidden image of God rose burning to the surface of his face. His was a stormy face anyway, one that both caught and revealed what was coming. He gazed at her with a shrug repeating. Her face turned coldly aside and then she fixed her stare on me accusingly.

The Brahmin of Great Pride in India was a very learned person who could juggle manifest and unmanifest and also could articulate questions belonging to the Western religious traditions. He rode around on a donkey but had an extra dose of pride which one day spilled out of him screaming. It dropped alive into hell. People saw that pride fall and the way the Brahmin immediately became like one of them at last.

Confucius thought nine times before speaking. Was each time identical to make up the nine? And the Duke of Chou held up his hair three times in his bath and spat the food out of his mouth three times during a meal. Everything that has form is also a mathematical secret and has to move very quickly to avoid being solved. I told my children that pride is the most dangerous quality of all. A little too much of it and you bring the house down.

A blind man whispered to me that people were afraid of him and he came to church only because the conscience of the people was roused enough to exchange words with him. Otherwise everyone on earth would hurry by, addressing the ground. He said his parts didn't add up. "People are body parts. Where is the whole body? Is sight a sensation? Can it be separated from the rest of the signs?"

I think nothing is either conscious or unconscious. If you want to be fully awake while you're asleep, wash both of your hands thoroughly before bed and anoint the left one with water of lilies. Write a prayer on this same hand and sleep on your right side. You will be like someone editing their own video in a dark room, during the dream.

"I want to try it, I want to try it!" cried Libby. "But what is water of lilies? Do you mash up the stems?"

Westerners fear what is out of sight and like to think that people know what they are doing even while they are not doing it. Darwin and Freud assumed that individuals and creatures at some level select the being that they become – they invent themselves.

"Otherwise, why does something bad feel so good?" Libby wonders.

In the good old days politicians either beheaded you or sent you into exile – they were considered equal forms of punishment.

Mimi loved me but didn't want to see me with Lewis whom she loved more. I loved Mimi, Libby, Lewis and three of my foster children. Libby didn't love Lewis but she slept with him. I loved Lewis and didn't. She did love McCool but I had his body. He loved her but felt guilty because he never loved me and never gave me children. I loved him three times but it wasn't enough for any of us. Lewis could have loved Libby if he had dared but he didn't. He sort of loved me but was afraid to be seen with me. "Old story. We were trying to become something new."

11-7

Soon Libby in her learning wanted to practice Tantric sex. She was a healer by then and a good one, her fingers crossed skin like a bird on sand, not digging in but dotting the top with spots of energy.

She suffered over the existence of violence in the world, it made her ill. She believed that men wasted their energy in orgasms when they should have held it in and let that energy coil up the spinal cord instead. Too much released turned them dry and violent. Rape camps in wars used the same energy as that used in killing, maiming and hating, according to Libby. Like that Brahmin of Great Pride, their excess went straight into hell-hate.

In order to teach Tantric sex, she needed to practice it herself, but she had no boyfriend and wanted one less. She was therefore interested in starting with Lewis because of his condition and because they had already been through their affair. Paralysis of the lower body with the life continuing in his genitals and most of his spine. She asked my permission soon after he and I finished work on our film.

"Kundalini yoga uses posture, breathing and meditation to raise your energy, send it up the psychic centers of the spinal cord into your brain," she explained. "This is part of the Tantric practice. It would be really good for Lewis. Someone has been teaching me. It's called 'being poured into the moonglass of pure consciousness.' Isn't that beautiful? Breath control is very important. I'd have to train him in that. The trick is to have an orgasm backwards really, to preserve the semen, or female energy. It would be really good for him, I think. He has so much anger in him. It's an ancient practice, thousands of years old. There's nothing intimate about it, I promise."

"But it's not for me to give you permission," I said. "As long as you don't kill him, I don't care what you do to him." "You're cross at me," she said. I convinced us both that I was not.

Lewis agreed to give the experiment a try saying he felt like stone. The plan was for her to arrive bearing perfumed water, honey, ointments and enough liqueur for both of them for weeks. She had been taught by a master who had her sit astride him while he was in the lotus position. He would barely penetrate her and remain erect for one to two hours while she practiced working her vaginal muscles and breathing in unison. She spoke of it with some reverence between roars of laughter. She was like many thin women – without strong sexual content but with a big longing.

"I've noticed," she said, "that the rich who exercise self-denial walk a little stiffly and are dry. The poor who are thin from starvation are ready for anything."

Libby was apocalyptic in her approach to the news and her days, and she believed in signs and portents while being very well informed in an ordinary way about the news of the world. Her fear of endings was greater than her desire for anything. Her kindness was greater than that fear, however, and she believed she could help Lewis feel happy again. "Where there's life, there's hope," she said like the medical establishment. "His grumpy male energy has to have somewhere productive to go," she added. "Believe me, I don't find him attractive at all. I can feel how blocked he is. I know he can be tyrannical, and look at him—he's all messed up physically."

During the first days she only massaged him. They sipped on creme de menthe or Bailey's and reminisced. He asked her if I was jealous. She said no, and then, "McCool would be jealous though."

"Because of me or because of you?" he wanted to know.

"He's never met you."

"No, but he hates me."

"Because Henny loves you."

"Do you think I should run off with her in the end?" he asked.

"Have you ever thought of that?"

"I am thinking about it now. No one else would want me."

"Not true," she assured him.

"Well, someone would–for my money or my fame. She's the only one who would love me."

"I don't believe that, but I think you should run off with her, whatever that means."

"We would go live together on an island somewhere."

"Why didn't you do it earlier?"

"She knows why," he said, as Libby reported to me later.

He lived in a luxury building. He was high up overlooking the harbor. This time Libby had bought hard pillows for them both and did some yoga exercises at the foot of his wheelchair before helping him onto the floor. Old Ironsides, she said and did a little ventriloquism for fun. He was laughing then. She said later that his heaviness was beyond measure and she felt dizzy after helping him get down. The whole time she feared getting him up again, or being unable to, and her breathing became spasmodic, she felt pains in her groin, she ignored them. He was more broken than she had imagined. They sat on the floor. His legs were awkwardly placed and she tried to lift them, was dizzy again. They were laughing together by then, the laughter that runs through a river of humiliation, and is a weeping from the mouth. The Egyptians called the iris of the eye a "mouth." Eye goddesses had suns in their mouths.

Istar was a big-eyed goddess like many others in the Canary Islands, Ireland, Malta, Greece, Crete, Cyprus, Anatolia and Syria.

They couldn't look each other in the eye while she kneaded between his outstretched legs and helped him slide back to the wall and then they rested. She unbuckled, unzipped and drew down his pants to give him freedom and took off her own pants. They both wore white underwear. She turned on some Indian music she had brought along but nothing soothed the pain in her groin. She loved the room they were in, the deep white wall to wall carpeting, the glass tables and big leather furniture, the framed awards, the paper flowers and other signs of fame and fortune. They convinced her she was safe. So she could attribute her dizziness to his weight and relax. He lacked kindness, though he was thoughtful from intelligence. He knew a person was as alive as he was, and just as feeling, but he felt no particular sympathy for their plight. He was hard. But behind the buddha-like bronze of his face, she saw more metal and then none, but a kind of opening, like a vault with a red stain at the base of it. He watched her with cold amusement. "What are you going to do with me next?" he asked. "I thought this was about sex."

"Don't worry, it is," she said blurring.

"So? Go for it."

She moved on her knees and placed herself across his lap, her face facing his, her breathing uneasy. "But you need the right attitude," she told him.

"Well, give it to me, that's your job."

This was despair they were both stinging with. They neither wanted this nor that. "You have to open up," she said dully. Then he pushed her roughly into it, making fun of her tantric fantasy, despising her pity for him. He forced her onto him, to raise him from his own humiliation. It wasn't special, sustained or pleasurable, and she was miserable, increasingly in pain where he pressed himself up in her, laughing. Her agony he took as joy, because she didn't tell him otherwise. Instead she went home as soon as she could after leaving everything, including him still half-dressed on the floor beside his wheelchair. At home in her own bedroom, she collapsed and within days learned she had cervical cancer.

11-8

The house was long, the rooms were crowded. My father had visited me in the last dream on the right – just before the back door out to the porch, and he had moaned about his difficulty with traveling through that space and how heavy his bags were. It was his way of explaining why he had been gone so long and I assured him "no more trips to the airport" which made him relax, smile and call I love you to my receding back. The dead grow in stature as time passes. Their personality intensifies becoming a scent. They seep into the faces of passers-by and emerge out of trees and restaurants in dreary new forms.

One evening Charlotte Bronte was wandering around Brussels in a state of profound despair and loneliness. She heard the bell from Ste. Gudule tolling vespers. And she, who despised Catholicism, though her grandmother was Irish Catholic, dipped into the church and wandered about watching old women saying their prayers. She stayed. She was paralyzed by her depression. Then she noticed several people entering the confessionals and she sat close by, watching.

Weirdly, as she wrote to her sister Emily, "I felt as if I did not care what I did, provided it was not absolutely wrong, and that it served to vary my life and yield a moment's interest. I took a fancy to change myself into a Catholic and go and make a real confession to see what it was like." Amazingly, she did exactly that. She told the priest she was a Protestant, he hesitated, but then urged her to make her confession anyway. And, she said, "I actually did confess a real confession." For some reason she compared her feelings at that moment to being alone on the Thames at midnight. But when the priest invited her to come to see him the next day, she said she would, knowing she wouldn't. And, she warned Emily, "I think you had better not tell papa this."

11-9

Blindness is often considered a punishment for seeing, which is like knowing. The blind, people think, must know something to deserve such an obvious mark of punishment. For instance they might have looked too intensely at something. People fear having the same thing happen to them, and think blindness might somehow be catching, so they don't look blind people in the eye. On the other hand, they think blind people might be more gifted than sighted people because they live in a world of darkness but continue to function. So maybe they should be worshiped and touched because of the miracle of their knowing anything at all. Many emotions follow blind people, so maybe it's lucky they can't see. Blind people are like souls without bodies, I've heard it said. They seem to have seen enough and to be saying, "No more!"

"But of course that's ridiculous," Tom commented.
"How can so many bad things have happened to one little boy?" I asked him.
"One thing leads to another. They are indivisible. I mean, the way things happen is not in a random sequence full of gaps."
"Why can't a relative of hers take care of him?"
"There's just a decrepit grandmother in Italy."
"But that doesn't make him my problem."
"You're right about that," said Tom, opening up his car and standing back to watch the boy approaching with his red-tipped stick in one hand and a book in the other.

Lewis was in his usual rush getting into his car. I looked away from them all at the wintery trees pressed on a pink slab of cloud. Then I called to Lewis, "Wait."

Lewis was crashing wheels, chairs and doors open and shut.
"You gotta adopt that child," he told me. "I'll help you," he added, "I promise. I'll pay for help or whatever."
"Why?"
"Well, it will keep us close. Almost married." He beamed

his smiling face at the sun to see my reaction.

"I don't believe in adoption," I told him.

"Well, foster, or whatever, but consider him ours. I'll pay for everything."

"But why?"

"I just said. We can pretend we had him. Say yes."

I refused to say yes, but my eyes must have said it because he called, "Settled!" before driving away. I noticed he had not promised anything.

There are children just like the god of happiness who dance around and don't let you touch them and run away just as you grab, but there are adults too who leave people soon after they say the one thing you always wanted to hear and those are the people you remember, I don't know why. The gesture seemed like a sister to suicide. There was a wipe-out imperative behind it that unnerved me.

11-10

This strange interruption in the scheme of things – this sudden journey to Ireland – is hard for me to explain. But one day Tom – in a little rented car – is driving me and Julio me past the Slieve League to see my grandmother in Donegal. She lives in a cottage set apart from a V-shaped road, from cliffs. She can catch a glimmer of water from a window in each room facing west. Her view is in the kitchen and she sits there all day staring at the aluminum gleam on the salt water. She squints at it. She is big like me but bent like a stuffed animal and her white hair is as thin as cotton and her white features fallen into a set of lumps. She has whiskers. Weirdly she knows a lot about me, remembers the details, pours us some decent tea, and asks after my mother and is clearly glad she is dead. Tom is very tall in the little rooms that are smelly and warm. He moves Julio around protectively, and takes him everywhere with him. Now he crashes with his cup and saucer on the edge of a couch reading *The Irish Times* while Julio hangs out an open window listening to the birds.

My grandmother wonders why it took so long for me to visit her. She had written me months before telling me that she was leaving me a little cottage she owned. "I didn't believe you," I explain. She tells me that American women have no faith and are driven by greed and ambition and are not as intelligent, brave or gentle as Irish women. This reminds her that I am married to a supposed Irishman and she grumbles then asks where my husband is. "We live separately," I tell her and she responds with a story, narrated in a smoker's husky and intimate tones.

"I once knew a woman who grew up in Purgatory. She met and married an atheist, a man she thought was good despite his lack of faith. But he was always taunting her for being foolish, until one day an angel floated down and sat on his head. When he reached up to bat it off, he found a crown of thorns in his hair. Now this is the truth. When he turned around to look at his wife, he was a new person, he had changed his tune. She saw it right away in his features, which had been twisted and now were smooth... And after that, they had several children, each one of whom they baptized. You might think about their example, darling."

"But example of what? Did he convert?" I asked. "I don't get the message." "Yes, it was a conversion," she said.

I heard Tom laugh in the other room and wanted to explain him to her before I had to leave her gazing out at the distant tinny water. But really she seemed not to care about him or why I had come at all until she told me to open a drawer in a chest in the livingroom and to take out a packet of photographs.

There was an old orange paper that held together a few treasured papers—two birthday cards signed "John"– one very old card signed "Mother"– my baptismal certificate from a Catholic church in Donegal years before, and an old wedding photo of me and McCool. There was also an old photo of my father as a teenager outside a tumbledown cottage. He was skinny and nervously smiling under his shade of hair. The other one of him in an army uniform I had seen before. She stabbed at the picture of my young father and said, "That's the cottage. That's now yours. Please don't sell it." She looked at me through filmy eyes and I cried and promised and helped her sit down. Tom was watching all this with his over-sensitive expression, and said, "We must go there at once."
"Did I really get baptized, Granny?" I asked her.
"What do you mean 'really'? Of course you did. Right at St. Patrick's, the way it's written there on the certificate. Take it

with you." And then she suddenly focused her face on Tom and Julio.

"Who are those people with you?" she asked me.

"They don't look American."

"They are. Just friends, Granny. The little boy – well, I am taking care of him."

"Poor thing. Bring him for a blessing. To Knock. Bring him, darling." Her words rolled around like fog on the rocks. She tipped her head and lowered her eyes when she spoke. The room had a loamy turf smell that only then did I notice. I went down on my knees and kissed the insides of her hands. "There's no time for that," she said. I looked into her face and saw my fate behind it. A cluster of genetic traits. Madness, included.

Tom and I drove for hours along the coast down from Connemara through Galway, along the cliffs of Moher, to Ennis. Just below there, near the water and Bunratty Castle, we found the cottage, in need of repair. So she wasn't a liar. The house was packed out of gray stone and stood in unshepherded fields not far from the highway to the airport. "Isn't it great? My mother lied. I was baptized," I informed Tom so softly he didn't hear me.

Instead he followed me through the rooms talking: "Have you heard of such a thing as saving history, or salvation history? Don't laugh. It's the history of revelations – not just the famous ones like Isaiah and Moses – or like the women saints Cecilia, Agnes, Felicity, Anastasia, Lucy –

Simone Weil at Solesmes – but ones that are unrecorded and obscure. A negative history in a way. I think these revelations are like gusts of wind that fill the sails or winds that hold up planes and birds – utterly invisible but buoyant and strong–fillers! – resting places – inns – negative only in the sense of their being empty rather than written, or material – the history of these spaces glue together the narrative of the world and pass through certain people, unarticulated – they save us all – they come from the other side of the cross – resurrective, you might say – oh well–hard to explain –"

"Why are you thinking about that now?"

"I don't know. Those cupboards need to be rebuilt."

"When I get back here…. Look. Julio loves it. I think in some way my granny was telling me that the resurrection is erotic. An erection bursting up out of the dirt. All red, fertile. I mean, in her story about the woman from Purgatory."

"You think so? Well, there might be something to that. Once Jesus has been through hell, his rising can only be associated with re-birth, sex, excitement of the flesh."

"The whole house needs rebuilding and repainting. Too bad McCool."

We stepped out the back door into a puffy wind, it is spring, Julio is standing under a large oak tree listening. The birds are rioting. "What will we do?" I ask Tom.

"Go see Dublin and then go home."

"I wish we could stay," said Julio. "Listen!"

Tom has come all this way with Julio to see if I can really take care of him, be responsible for his safety, focus on all the issues that arise out of his not-seeing. I have almost committed myself to taking him home with me. His foster parents, like mine so many years ago, are very old and unable to care for him properly. This contributes to my feeling of inevitability about the arrangement. Coincidence, a likeness, producing a collapse of judgment.

Sometimes you walk up some stairs, or down a hall, and a person is standing there, as if waiting for you. They are at a desk, but on their feet; or next to a bookshelf, face down; or on a telephone, and they wave to you as you approach, they signal you in.

This sometimes seems like a supernatural encounter, like a coincidence – the person being there at the end of thousands of days of walking, seeking, slowing. I wonder if Julio feels that way about me. For instance, what if Mary and Jesus are the ones actually producing all those statues of themselves? What if they are reenacting the traumas of their own sorrows again and again through the hands of humans?

Julio is always between us like a given except when we are in our beds. That night, after driving across Ireland, Tom and I sneak away from him sleeping and meet alone in the comfy lobby of the Mount Herbert Hotel in Dublin where we are staying.

"Do you remember the the actress in *The Double Life of*

Veronique? I would run away with her in a minute," Tom says out of the blue.

"Irene Jacobs. You're kidding. I thought you didn't fall for women."

"Celibacy wouldn't mean much if I didn't want sex," he says impatiently. We have now mentioned both celibacy and erections in one day. But I don't dare carry the conversation further. I am afraid to ask, directly, if he is gay. I already know that he hated his mother, had a half-brother, his father was a communist, and he had loved someone sort of.

"But who do you want it with, besides Irene Jacobs?" I start to ask but begin to quarrel with him instead, as if I have to make small-talk to keep his attention off an absent object of desire.

The subject of politics is a perfect one for fueling an alternative excitement and there are Germans wandering around us, speaking loudly and looking out the windows at the grey evening light that lasts for hours in Dublin at this time of year.

But I have no words. At that hour Libby is still alive in America. Lewis is too. The children I raised have grown and gone. I stare out the window into the blackening silhouettes of trees. A gold-rimmed cloud floats by, illuminating leftover raindrops. The candescence of each spot of water turns one twig into a rhinestone chain. The birds are very strong of voice, their notes are strung with nearly robust pleasure. And I am there to face the fact that I will never be loved by anyone on earth but children.

11-11

"What is the course of the cosmos? Is it Brahman? From where do we come? What do we live by?" the Upanishads are good enough to ask out of the mystery of making choices.

What is a mother if not a body that has manufactured and produced another body? All the parts are literally parts – broken off, one from the other, severed, ripped, removed by force. The day itself and the trees planted in space are broken off from other ones just like them, are scattered objects too.

The mother – and almost any woman can be one if she wants – has undergone the ordeal of being physically broken – has had a living part ripped off of her. The mother who lives somewhere separate from her child – is she still a mother? Is the everlasting fragmenting of nature into bits and pieces a motherly act? Are all women mothers-to-be, even the little ones who hate children and the old ones who never had them? Why do so many people hate their mothers? There are institutions that exist for battered and abused children. There are foster families like mine who take them in for money. These welfare buildings that are broken into spaces are like inns in the mind of God – way stations for wounded children, mansions in the brain of time. Words are interruptions in an eternal moan. When a deaf child speaks slowly, you know how slowly you yourself speak, breaking into the long note with stammers punctured with air. I think Lewis is right. All of us carry the same genetic imprint, but in a specific individual, the imprint has specific exaggerated features. I think he is right, that every baby is like any baby. But I know, too, that there is some strange extra force that draws you to one child and not to another—some recognition that is like a magnetic field. A fate. The feel, the smell, the weight of the child – these are properties that have great intrinsic power of their own, and make each child special, each one different, each one lovable to one person and not to another. Never to meet a child you love like that – this would be a real sorrow. Fortunately, as you know, God, you can meet a child who is as close to you as your own would be; fortunately for both of you because it is unmistakable.

The word "mother" is meant to be associated with love and care-taking that follows giving birth to a child. But it also means the love and the care-taking as processes in themselves. Therefore a father can be a mother. At its best, the point of the word "mother" is that it is a quality, not a condition or a situation. So let's say "motherer" instead of mother.

These types are treated badly often, abandoned or exploited. For a while their children reward them with love and kisses, but then the children, like burdens, cause them pain. You have to learn to want nothing in return for anything you do, in order to be an ideal mother. Ideal as in irreproachable and independent. I think that a motherer could be a very positive role-model in our society if she or he really developed its qualities into revolutionary ones. But this person would still have to love—in a fatal way—someone else. Child, baby, or full-grown person.

Why? A motherer is willing to die for the other and she or he is more independent in her spirit than anyone who doesn't love. She has eliminated the desire for rewards by the time she is a real motherer. And of course this is the essence of liberation because it is the opposite of what society wants people to want. If you had a society of motherers who didn't care if they died, who had no interest in rewards, and who just wanted to play all day, what would happen to this world?

11-12

McCool roamed and returned and roamed and returned like a bird wired for my nest. Wherever I went, he was soon on the phone or following. His unrelenting presence was the only evidence I had in my life that there might be a karmic system at work after all.

He was down to wine and bread in the end and raving. I put a mattress for him on the front porch or grass wherever I lived when the ground was either wet or cold.

One night he told me his true childhood story through a crack in the raised livingroom window. "I grew up in Virginia. My mother was crazy and ran off with a black dude, an electrician, and somebody dumped me in a foster home where the only nice person was Irish. I got my Irish passport because my grandma was Irish but dead. I'm scared the black dude might have been my dad. I mean, who knows. I mean, it's obvious. I mean, I'm not."

I didn't tell him that I already knew he was a liar. I slammed down the window.

"I love you, I love you" was all Libby could say to anyone, her shadow ripped like road kill where she hung halfway out of her bed. "I don't want to die!" was written in her eyes. But you HAVE to. You CAN'T have what you want, her body replied. It was this same body's resistance to her desire to live that brought about the supernatural transformation in her final being. She couldn't even pretend she could have what she wanted. And so she turned into a saint, right in front of my eyes.

"At least you have done something with your life," she kept insisting.
"Making videos of dreams is a useless occupation," I swore to her. "Instead I wish I had known this earlier. When you run out of ideas, become an activist, take care of things, or be a prophet who has visions. Don't get depressed."

Now she wanted to travel though she was very ill. She wanted, in particular, to visit the compound on the canyon, and so I flew with her there to stay for three days. She had oxygen and morphine, two muu-muus to wear, a cap for her bald head, and she only consumed mangoes and tea during that time. She was scared of anything physical coming close and damaging her skin. Insects, splinters, torn leaves and thorns in the bougainvillea. I had to take walks alone while she sat in sunlight wrapped in a black and orange muu-muu, rocking on a walkway between bedroom and kitchen. We tested our memories; identified things like stars and flowers; and reminisced. She slept early, breathing badly, on a twin bed beside mine. During that time she told me about McCool and she cried at her cruelty to him.

She showed me the strength of his building – weirdly distanced from my own observation – techniques. The thick stilts, the strong carved cupboards, the varnished floors and walls, the details around the windows. How hard he had labored hammering, measuring, lifting, sanding, all with belief that they would live there for good. "He was even nice to my kids—took them to school and picked them up on time. Did a lot of the cooking. Oy vey! Och! Ach du lieber Augustine! Mein Gott! How could I have been so cruel?"

I walked the planks and inspected walls and rooftops and admitted that this was a good job indeed that he had done, the rough look of it was deceiving. "He grew up on a farm, building with his dad, he told me," Libby explained. "He said they were starving poor, black Irish."

"Right. Well, he must have been happy here with you."

"Then why do I feel guilty?"

"You always do," I told her.

"No, it was bad. I got bored. But he was so good in bed, you know, being infertile made him seem like an angel.

Literally. I could be completely free. But he wasn't famous. He was a loser, let's face it, and all I ever wanted was a famous man. You know that. It's why I'll go to hell!" She bawled in tiny meek gasps, and I felt a sensation in my left temple that had come and gone for decades. It was the kind of pain that lets you know what it is to be a piece of wood being sawed. That is, it was not exactly pain in the usual human sense, more of a final sensation – a rush of too much energy. I pressed it, staggered, dizzied, then sat beside her. She didn't notice any of this but pressed her mouth into the flesh of an open mango I held out to her. The Hindu orange of the fruit against her face restored her soul's transcendence, and we smiled. She now made a monkey face, then shut her mouth and threw the word, "Yum" into the palm trees overhead. I had no impulse to say the perfunctory: "Don't feel guilty." Because I realized that remorse was what had made her a saint.

I have learned that people often get very ill, or even die when someone they love is dying, but they don't connect the one thing with the other. They just get mad at themselves for being sick at such an important time. The blood vessel burst in my left temple when Libby was in her last days. I was hospitalized, became comatose, was operated on, survived, just in time to receive the white flowers Libby sent me two days before she died. I only heard, then, about her sublime exit, her words as she slipped away: "Henny, you would not believe it," and her cremation on a snowy Massachusetts day.

TENSE

The present tense is depressed because it pretends that it can extend out to either side; that it can catch a fact as a series of words lined up in the same sentence. The past tense is calm since everything it expresses is already over. The past tense soothes its words into inertia until squalor becomes the past's natural habitat. That's why the past is the future of religion. Religions are fertile like garbage coming alive too. The over-now of the past haunts religion – mourning makes all the people stand up and sing.

The sweeping gloom of a church's interior hides the dead in the galleys while the people who pray are on deck and lighted. The dead in religion are its foundation, its energy base.

Monastic life is orderly and thoughtful but many people think it is a lazy, useless way of life. Every person has the potential to be a monk or solitary but only a few tend to develop it because it is so difficult and despised. Repetitious days, prayers, no results. What for? I think the imitation of the clock is a useful practice for all humanity to learn from, and the seed of revelation is buried in the monastery as is the salvation of the contemporary church.

As for the rest, the tenses should be graphically written in columns with the past on the left column, the future on the right, and the present across from the writer's throat where the heart pulses out of and into the past simultaneously. Out of, or in to? How can these be the same action? The dead inhabit the bodies of the living coming and going at will. The will is synonymous with the spirit and the spirit with time. The heart belongs to gurus. And God is as absolutely elusive as memory. It is fleet. It is elusive as in allusive. It is a carrier and an evaporator. Memory is God.

The dead have abandoned the bodies of the living to the world like mothers who leave their children. The dead have taken off in search of deep time. They have no feelings left for the living, or they refuse to tell the living what they really felt for them while they were all alive. This mystery is almost too much to bear for those left languishing on the top of the ground.

You must try to replace the dead who dropped you with someone else who will at least tell you how they feel about you before it is too late.

What is death but something related to faith?

Faith has experience but doesn't want to stop there. Faith knows that getting what you desire is disappointing. Faith converts that realization into a big angry shove against the facts. To have nothing in the way is the prayer of the truly faithful. Faith sounds optimistic but its roots are angry, its stem is impatient, its flower furious. Faith becomes a ghost-shape of the thing it once was, when it lived in a baby. Old faith turns a cold shoulder to new people.

I don't trust faith but I don't trust hope even more. I can't stop hope any more than I can quiet my mind. Meditation

is the end of hoping and I can't meditate because I can't sit
still and stop hoping. God hates me. I am someone who
failed to be whole-hearted at loving God or others. I should
have died for something by now. I know this is true but I
hope that I am asking too much of myself. I know that I am
a failure in this world. I should have been discovered to be
worthy otherwise. I still hope I will be. The only thing I have
in common with God is that I don't exist. Nobody sees my
films or my body.

If they say God is love, I don't know what they mean by
love, though I know what they mean by God. I have seen
terrible things that a loving and powerful God, who was like
a parent, would simply not allow to happen. I hate it when
they give God attributes. God is not love or memory.
God is as plain as its meaningless name.

I don't admire haters, though I know some, and I do know
what hate is myself, and God is not hate, but may have hate.
God is not love unless it is everything else too. People
admire haters and want to follow them wherever they go.
A hater can be a great leader. Hate seems as honest as it
isn't.

To believe in something means to understand it. I wonder
if the reason haters can be great artists is that they put so
much good into their work that the extra goes to making
hell for everyone else. Why not do that after all if there is
no Christ to be the best critic. Why worry about people's
feelings unless you are either superstitious, or nationalistic.

History is not a help, the way knocking wood is. It is not fair. We all share one God in our imagination and it makes our one mind.

Most people are not famous or nation-conscious but live little difficult lives kissing other people in case they are left alone like old mothers. The stones that people raised into buildings are beautiful. Anonymously lifted in a communal enterprise that the dead who plied them can be proud of. They aren't. They died and walked away, bored. How do I know this. The dead are disgusting and the dead are divine.

They carry attributes for a while with them and then become slime and/or sky. I don't understand them. I don't believe in them. I hate them. They are often mean-spirited when they return, glueing their eyes to you. They whine about their problems with travel. Yet, in spite of this, I don't mind dying and joining them. Not that there is a choice. But the world and living can be at odds. Only religion, while I am alive, can span the two conditions. Ask God. The sanctuary is the space that opens into death.

You dream of releasing a pack of aging, mangy dogs and cats from a pound and then not wanting them. This is what the sanctuary does not do. It does not release into your care the mouldering and miserable travelers from the next world. Their greeds and hesitations are not your business here. The sanctuary is like the back room of an alchemist's shop where the powdering and polishing go on. It wants to make things shine so the dead won't be able to see their way in. Rock crystal, citrine, copper, sapphire, ruby, violet, pale yellow amethyst, moonstone, opal, garnet, black and gold. I always come back to movies, paintings, ikons and music and how much hangs on them. A lot hangs on me and my never getting what I want, too. Withholding is holding. I withhold too much. Now I know nothing but the sentence of St. Bridget interests me. She blinded herself rather than get married. If she was the man I think she was, she promised herself nothing in order that others might live. This is not a joke. I too fear my happiness would destroy the world. If I allowed myself to desire and to fulfill my desire, the fragile alliances between people I love would falter and fail. They would grow ill, get hurt, lost. God keeps me from demanding anything strongly enough to get it. Why is it only me who has to make this path, you might ask in disgust at my whining. There are plenty of others who do too, believe me. We don't talk about it because people would laugh at us. In parks you see many of the people who have what they want because it isn't much. There, ducks honk like children's toys when the batteries are weak. I think the most admirable people on earth are the activists who take care of the poor. What I don't like about the dead is the size of their secret. It covers them completely. They turn inside out is what I don't like. We are always dying but we are never dead. The dead don't believe they are dead because a word like "dead" means non-existent and words only apply to what exists. That's why they don't understand what has been said when you use that word and they keep talking about being late and missing trains. One of them just looked at me from his youth unhappily as if to present his majesty in the role of tragedy. Never has one I knew returned radiant as in resurrected. Mary returns because she can't get over what the world did to her child. She is like one of those traumatized ghosts who still believe they are alive and completing a task.

Mary knows that people have made images of her suffering in a terrible world. She knows that some of us understand her. Nothing can comfort her as a mother. She comes again and again, saying "This didn't happen!" holding her baby up. She carries that baby everywhere.

Sometimes you see with the dead that it is all inside out. The sheet that is drawn over the secret inner body of the person is stripped away and you see what was buried but living all along. These are the recent dead. Some of the dead just evaporate. But the dead of God are like fiery beings, who can adapt to the freezing skies, happy bodies of transparent light, balls of colors you can see through.

They dance. They are joy. They don't take up space like balloons although they resemble them. They don't waste time. They have been ground to a powder, then a color. Annihilated. They swirl in front of and over you. They don't get cold, don't worry. They only want to assure you that they are fine. Their message is: have no fear. There are no secrets among the dead of God because they are God. Except God does not exist any more than Dead does. This is why there are no names for it or them when they have gone to God. God's inexistence is so deep, black and big, there is no way to see or name it. God is inert. Why bother with it then. What does it have to do with anything that does exist. In fact it is your own business if you want to bother with it or not. God doesn't care if you understand it or not, or talk to it or not. God stays quiet. That is all you can say. In the end, that's what you like about it. But you can choose to try to understand God in the meantime for your own sake. Just be realistic. When you can't enter and describe something, it is called unrealistic and fantastic. Unrealistic is confused with "not real." It is much easier to predict what will happen to people who choose evil than to predict what will happen to good people who suffer unjustly.

When I say God wants me to do something I don't mean that God is saying Do it, do it from somewhere. I don't hear voices or see angels.

I mean God is God and the godness of all being in all time gods that godness gods to God God greets God because it is already God, the rest is colorless.

I am a crackle of static between God and God… motion without color. The dead of God, who are they? How do we know which ones turned into worms and which ones into the sky tolerating the quiet in their house, the blindness in their eyes, the losing of their senses, the cold and absence of gravity? Who dares to not fear? Who dares to not land somewhere?

Who dares to ride between all things forever like the chirp

from a bird's beak before it finds an ear? I don't know who they are. I don't know who God is, godding inside of me. Therefore I don't know who I am because I don't know where it will go when it comes out in the air.

Of what already happened I remember little though the parts remain dismembered in my godcells. God lives like a dream you forget. God are babies. God are beauty and ugliness. I remember God best when I feel worst. Explain this. Or my mother will because she was always complaining. When you break a real person, you break a little piece of God. The light whitens the pores of the person's skin, colding it, then it dies. I love you is the favorite message of the dying who have a chance to say it. The Beatitudes are great. They and the Upanishads are greater than any words except I love you. The Beatitudes understand the people and their suffering. They say how there are feelings that we all have in common, no matter where we come from and it reassures us for having feelings of hate, grief and littleness, for being remorseful and dry all in a mass.

At Mass they don't say that mourning for someone you loved is a happy thing because they wouldn't say "mourning" unless they really meant that you are intensely unhappy. But comforted how?

What he might mean is that mourning teaches you to love without an object.

Loved means pressed between God and God. Blessed means pressed there too. To not-know where the dead have gone and where, or if you will find them. It brings a discovery that all beauty is a geometry that is marked in relationship.

A blind singer said he couldn't describe blindness any more than you could describe color.

God-talk is nonsense since God is outside existence, so why can't we help it? Why can't we stop talking about it unless God is broken into words and God is not memory and God is not like memory. The Gospels are told in the past tense but after Isaiah who in some way made them. The year then ends with Christmas where it begins in retrospect and it begins at Easter where it ends in retrospect. Krishna, Moses, Ruth, Naomi and the Marys are great but Jesus is the only one we ever hear about who really died. All the others might have just disappeared, gone elsewhere, even Socrates, and we will hook up with them later at some station or other. But you know that Jesus died because he returned and not with his usual face looking sad or angry but as a cheerful stranger walking down the road. Easter is when the earth is reborn and so is Jesus who really died as in "was changed."

The Gospels look back at resurrection from the vantage point of already knowing the Passion at the end of the year and knowing the whole story beginning with the end.

If they didn't know the whole story already, they would not know what tense to use. Most human stories end before death. The people die to life. But they had the past all wrapped up together in a book. They could have left it carved on a stone, but wanted to turn pages, to show how it feels to see things multiplying and speeding by very fast, then also being preserved and contained between covers. Words carved on top of a stone would not convey the way God is always in the present because God is always present so you can be confident of speaking of God as something that speeds past and gets lost simultaneously or vice versa. What is sad to discover is that events in this world are both pre-determined and whipped up at the moment they are occurring. People are bewildered by this paradox unless they can grasp the difference between time and timing. It is like the way they write out their calendar make predictions and watch events unfold according to plan.... and then it all goes wrong and a choice becomes necessary.

The choice seems to exist outside of the layout of time; there seem to be no precedents for what they have to decide. Has the result already happened? Is the choice going to affect all of history?

This is what is shocking about the story of Jesus whose life was prophesied down to its end and who nonetheless confused everyone when the prophecy was coming true. Peter had to make a big decision already knowing what the result of his decision would be. He failed three times anyway. He acted as if his life would be saved by remaining silent. This might have been the first time that determinism and free will came into slam-conflict, setting off earthquakes an eclipse and a resurrection. Too confusing even for the heavens.

This must be why everything depends on how you place yourself in a book. The crucifixion is a kind of Christmas if the narrators already knew that he would be walking around on the next page. However, if they started with the resurrection, and left out his crucifixion, then you would not be sure he really died. Only having the resurrection directly follow the crucifixion proves that he died. I just wish it all could have begun with the resurrection and none of that suffering of mother and son had to happen at all.

Still, I better be glad that he really died because then I know something about one person that makes sense. You don't know that the others died because they never came back. Something else must have happened to make them stay away so long.

Jesus went into hell for three days and discovered death for the first time. He had to die of course in order to discover where the dead went and report back to us. Virgil and Dante did this too but they weren't tortured getting there so it was fiction.

It was the discovery of the world. In the museum there is a picture of Jesus lying under flat stone with a light on.

Our ancestors believed that the dead took a journey and they left them food and flowers and had ceremonies to urge them on out. To Dis, Hades, the Elysian Fields, the Great Spirit, etc. They didn't expect to see them again. Meantime their gods were always elsewhere but on earth which may be why they didn't look at the sky for their metaphors. There was an underground god of geography to manage the arrangements for the after-life. The material fact is that we are already in heaven, every minute inside the sky. No wonder the Vatican has a telescope!

The resurrection threw all of us off because it proved that a person didn't necessarily go up on a trip but actually died down, the way it looks. There was an agony following a betrayal and torture, total loss of consciousness and a stone tomb. These happened to be death for Jesus because there he was three days later standing beside the same tomb they put him in. And he didn't look the same but was his soul. In the East there is a returning as someone else, too, after a long whirl through troubling eternities. But this returning isn't usually as fast or as site-specific as the resurrection though Milarepa did return soon to his devotees. It's more of a guess and a speculation by those avenging injustice. I myself believe that there is a system for sorting out the soul-cells according to quality and color and smell. This is why the eucharist is colorless, odorless, tasteless. It is trying to be nothing.

SNEAK AWAY TO MEDITATE

12.1

The moments seem to be what they are – a monument, a shrub, a ring, a hand, a foot – and to have no larger resting point, no gentle bounce in time. I am in Mount Auburn cemetery, on the peak of a small grassy knoll, where there is a sculptural semi-circle of marble, engraved with many names. Libby's will be chiseled there soon. But now there is a large crowd of friends assembled to say hello to her memory, and no officiating religious. Not even a saffron robed man is there. We all watch her children, now adults, place a black box in the ground, then back up. Grave-diggers, two cheerful men in a truck, lounge and smoke at a distance. Crematorium, if it were the name of a color, would describe the sky that day. The people sniff, pray, giggle, cough, whisper and gulp. But they are not articulate or boasting people, and have no ritual language for their New Age grief. Some start to lurch forwards, recitation on their lips, but back-step, shame-faced, and this superb failure of words, like an experience of mass cowardice, makes us enemies for a flash.

Even Lewis is there, but set apart at the intersection of Anemone Path and Orange Path. He has lifted himself out of his car and leans there where a stone says Roland O. His expression is unusually hard, the way eyes get when they stop in the middle-distance and see a reverie take shape. I, too, stand at a distance where I can see him and the hole in the ground through the legs of Libby's children's father. There are no leaves on the grass, though the trees are bare and crowing. The branches seem to speak through the black birds, to use them as emissaries for their mute wishes.

The sun is the color of a perfume in a transparent bottle. No one seems to know what to do, or when to turn to leave. I nod at Lewis whose smile lives alone in the air while I love it from afar. And in that moment I see the old silver car that belongs to my husband shooting like a bullet at the bunch of us. No, not a bullet. In retrospect a face made of steel, the silver teeth exposed and grinning. There is no noise.

Transparency of air has never been clearer and sound's dependency on no-sound for travel. Then screams and thumping, and then the car veers down Mound Ave. and off to the right, spins sideways for a few seconds, and continues away.

Lewis is hit. Wheels spinning like Gandhi's vision of productive village life. The people shrieking and shouting.

A coward's way of killing always resembles an accident. No one knows how to give the last rites, to say any words of consequence to him, but me, I have "I love you" on my lips and him held, though he's not there anymore. Soon I am speechless, clogged and swallowed, while the crows articulate the air's distress.

Some tepid green waters frogged at the bottom of a black and leafy hill. Many were born from Mother Sion – foreigners from Tyre and Ethiopia, among others who thought they had nothing in common. For half an hour we were strangers embracing and moving in a pack stinking of love and fear. Then this concentration thinned and the body was driven away in a van, Lewis was driven off into eternity.

Nobody but me knew what had happened and who had been driving the Honda. Everyone saw silver but each person thought it was a different model–a Mazda, a Saab, a Toyota, a Ford... so the police had unobservant witnesses that day. I didn't follow the body to the hospital but gave the police his family's name, though they were all the way off in Missouri. Then I went back to the little apartment in the brick building, where Julio and I lived alone together. Old ice as gray as cobble stones was welded to the edging and knotted up in patches on the cement.

Maybe when humans arrived on earth their wings tore from their backs, the wind too strong for them. Sometimes I thought I heard the ghost of feathers dragging behind Lewis when he moved that contraption. I wonder why he was always held back from ordinary action and cold like armor, even before anything bad happened. He didn't say anything to explain it to me.

Instead a thin layer of pain swished around his skin, and I could sense it, when he turned and wiped his face, but I acted as if what I was perceiving was a white lighted feather between his fingers and not a handkerchief. Likewise he always left me in the folds of the building's shadows and only pretended to care about me and Julio.

Once, I remember, Lewis's knee kept jumping up and down and up and down in front of the white light. He couldn't get the right angle on the film that was reeling around the knobs. What to cut and what to keep, it was very late at night. No one else was in the studio but us. He would then stand here and stand there, behind my chair and beside my chair, back at the wall or hunched over the little screen where the image was projected. I began to experience the air as a kind of toxin, the way it feels inside an MRI or some medical machine that is scoping out your interior.

Charged particles are black on the outside with light inside. Spit on a glass under a microscope will wobble like kaleidoscopic pebbles. Semen too swims at high speed, poliwogs on alert. We liked what we saw. Striped pajamas, a grey bar motel. Lewis liked it so much, he reacted as he always would to a woman at his side. He ran the side of his hand down the slide of my spine, until his palm flattened down and pressed my buttocks. We weren't in jail after all. So I pressed back into him at last and lay upright on the air, leaning, he might have been my bed. We were still young, my children were at home, while his hands moved around and onto my breasts, his face in my neck and my laughing. Then we couldn't stop hugging and kissing until we were down on the floor and our knees, necking. And up again, he was as agile as a lamb, with me saying I love you and him saying, "Me.... too.... you." And then it was over as fast as it started, and without more of an acknowledgment than a smile, we were soberly commenting on the cuts we must make. This would be our most intimate hour, in retrospect a black speck, a shell with a lighted interior, some atomic center, potential and immanent, transcendent and hot.

Augustine says that when you love, you are what you love, and so you love nothing, since you are nothing. When, therefore, the one you love dies, you don't physically die too, but you remain as you were in your love-state, before, when the person lived. You are incorporated into nothing-love.

Now anyone might think that McCool would finally vanish from my life after the hit-and-run. I certainly didn't turn him in, just in case I was wrong, let's say. But then I moved very quickly, because I really had nothing much left to say to anyone, not even Tom. I had already left my house and rented an apartment for me and Julio beside the river and nearer to the school for the blind. Tom formulated some plans for when to head north to the monastery and visited me infrequently, perhaps afraid of a mourning state that was outside of language. But McCool had no such fear, as I should have known, and found me.

12-2

He arrived, wet-coated and cold and stinking of gin. He might as well have been wearing handcuffs on his outstretched red hands. After all, what is repentance in solitude?
I let him in, and led him, obediently, to the bathroom first, so he could vomit and shit, and then to his closet. I made

sure he had a chamber pot, a bottle of water, peanut butter and a box of crackers. The closet was plumped up with old coats and shoes, boxes of tools, paint, and a flashlight he could use. He slipped right in and sat down, sobbing, and we said the Lord's Prayer together before I shut and locked the door. Soon enough McCool was dubbed the Bumper by the boy because of the noises he made. For three days he banged around that closet, without any method I could interpret from the sounds. He was, in a sense, a musician without an instrument. The closet was a sound studio maybe, as well as an orgone box, a confessional booth, and a safe-house. Whatever he did in there, he didn't try to break free when I changed his water or emptied his chamber pot. Instead he stayed meekly crouched in the dark still praying and shaking.

The superintendent complained of the banging. The old lady upstairs complained too. But it was only when Julio began to seem frightened that I left the door open so McCool could come out. He didn't. Instead he formed himself into a mound in the back corner where he repeated the Jesus Prayer, the Hail Mary, and even a prayer to Hamlet and to Libby.

I stood and watched him. Tinny bells were ringing from St. John the Evangelist, down the street, because it was noon. And I had to meet Tom.

A gold and oily sun lay on the city that day. The children were going on a field trip and stood around on the steps of a library, huddling where the sun felt warmest. Tom had brought them apples and cookies. "I've got a plane ticket to Montreal….We're going to have to say goodbye," he told me when the van drove away. We walked in the shade of bricks and ended up on the steps of St. John the Evangelist where I wanted to make a confession. "Can't I just make it to you, Tom? I mean, you're almost a monk, for God's sake."

He wouldn't let me. And laughing pushed me in through the door. The old priest with a lizard's lacy fingers was perfectly nice to me, but even after the blessing, I knew I was lost.

Tom and I dragged down the street together, with me poised to tell him about McCool, what he had done, and where he was hiding. Instead I asked him if he would do me a favor, later, without telling him what it was, and he nodded, perplexed, then went on his way as fast as he could.

Alone, I walked for blocks, noting the whiteness of a winter light on stones. A whiteness that was really a kind of thin gold, a just tone across the tops of things. I crossed the bridge and ran to catch lights, and hurried to a building I had only casually noticed from the car before. It was a dreary fifties-style Catholic church. And because it was Wednesday, confessions were going on there, too. Down a long hall, and not in a booth, I saw the priest standing by a bookshelf in a wooden room, and he turned and smiled and waved me in. He looked like Jonathan Winters — jolly and neurotic at the same time. His heart's face was flat, red and kind. Un-probing, he helped me through my first confession sitting in front of me like a psychiatrist with his hands splayed on his wide knees, his plump fingers drumming on a book he held there. He listened, and prompted me, my mouth was dry, then read to me about how when you are young you put on your own belt but later someone puts it on you and drags you somewhere you don't want to go. In fact, it was what Jesus once said to Peter: "I tell you most solemnly, when you were young you put on your own belt and walked where you liked; but when you grow old, you will stretch out your hands, and somebody else will put a belt around you and take you where you would rather not go."

After I had told the priest as much horrible stuff about myself as I could, he asked me if there was some valuable penance I myself could imagine for myself. I told him, "Not to talk holy-talk ever again."

"That's a good one!" he roared and laughed, patting his hands together. "A true conversion." Then he blessed me.

Rushing and puffing through the yellow air, all the way home, I pulled my hands through the air, as if it was strung with theories I was pulling down. This dream was called *The Holy Secular*.

At the little apartment I ran into my room and squatted on the threshold of the closet and looked inside. McCool was still there. He might have been the Hunchback of Notre

Dame, and me Esmeralda when she offered him a little sip of water and some kindness, up in the belfry. The bell-gongs seemed to come from inside the closet with him. I reached around him and took out the flashlight, and turned it on.

The closet had been transformed from a pitch dark and neglected site into a holy cave – gold iconic images were painted on the walls, faces of the Theotokos, the mother of God and her Son stared back at me, and angels spread white and red wings around them. INRI was written in red like graffiti across the back wall. The space had a poisonous metallic smell from the paint. "That's beautiful, McCool," I told him. "That's beautiful. But come on out now or you'll get sick." I moved back to the window to hear the rain wheeling upwards from the tires of passing cars outdoors, as if Ezekiel was sighing while his Merkabah visions hit the ground. Moans, regrets like the residual hiss of enormous winds billowing around the globe and making bells ring in all the steeples. McCool was full of regret. But he had made a closet into a sacred space. Into the place of his sobs and paintings were sucked the caws of crows, cars rushing, ice squeaking on the river, children's voices and dogs. He came out, saying "I didn't mean to, it was an accident."

I left the room and lost control of myself without using one sentence from a religious thinker. He might, after all, be telling the truth.

12-3

Julio, on the way home, asked, as he had asked many times before: "What happened to Lewis?"
"He was in a crash. You know that."
"I still don't get it. What does that mean?"
"A car hit him. Out of the blue.

The dusk was furry on the sycamores along the river. The brick arms of the building extended darkly out to us. "It's scary," said Julio. "Something comes and kills you."
"It's really scary," I agreed.
My hand lay lightly on his shoulder, we didn't have far to go, and he liked to walk remembering and counting and noting new effects. The cars sped by on our left. I told him, "The Bumper is out of the closet." "Who is it?"
"Just a man. You don't need to worry."
"What kind of man?"
"Good question."

When we entered the apartment, McCool was showering which struck me as obscene, and I stole his passport out of his bag. When I called Tom and told him that I needed him to do that favor now, he agreed to come over. He had been living in the Paulist Center and working with the homeless. Now he was aiming to go north at last.

The sound of McCool's voice speaking to the child made me gag.

"What does it feel like, being like you?" my husband was asking. "Blind."

"Well, I can always tell when Ma is coming, even when she is still outside," Julio answered. "It's not like hearing something special. I can't even say what it is exactly that lets me know. She does everything exactly on time, and maybe that's it."

"Undoubtedly…. She took you to Ireland?"
"Once and she gave me the names for things over there because she says she loves words."
"She does indeed."
"Leeks, pignuts, marjoram, mustard, a cuckoo, a bee, a chafter, wild goose, ducks, a wren and a woodpecker, a heathpoult and—um—heather, apples, raspberries and juniper, a lick of honey, a drop of rain and honeysuckle."
"Very pretty," said McCool in his Irish accent and punctuated it with a sob.
"We are going to design a garden for the blind in our new house."
"And I'm going to Ireland," said McCool.
The boy said softly: "You'll see. The birds are sharper and clearer and their songs have longer notes in Ireland."
"Is that so."
"They seem more awake than any birds I ever heard before."
"Really."
"I thought you were Irish," the boy remarked.
"Not any more….I mean, I will be soon. Again."

"Can you stop?"

The radiators banged. I only heard feet and breathing while I prepared their food, and my feelings were heavy as if there were black-loads of new blood dragging on the red. I went to the door hearing a moan, a sob, and the boy asking him – to cheer him up–

"Where does a bird keep its ears? You don't know? I only know now. Don't worry… I've made big mistakes too. I used to think that dogs had only two legs and a person's head was attached to its arms, extending out of the neck and the eyes were holes. I have never held a bird so I don't know where its ears would be. Ma says a tulip has four lives and in the last one it might as well be called a poppy. She tells me stories, folk ones and new – about sewing wings for swans and eating poison things, hiding fairies inside bottles and saving a forest, about *The Odyssey* and *The Iliad*. And she reads *Bambi*, *Pinocchio*, *The Wizard of Oz*…. aloud over supper. Do you like stories?"

No answer from McCool who had sunk into a chair, his hand over his eyes.

The boy slipped over and whispered in my ear: "I might not get what is happening. The Bumper doesn't seem like a man exactly. He seems to be a baby too. Is he? Maybe there are little people the size of porcupines that I can't touch. This is the main part that I don't get."

"Well, no wonder, I told him. I will explain later, after Tom gets here." I saw on his small smooth face a look of perplexity approaching fear.

"Everything will be fine soon."

The boy turned his face wonderingly towards McCool whose head was now between his knees. I could tell he wanted to reach out and touch that head to see what it was made of, but he politely resisted the impulse.

"Have you been to an airport before?" he asked McCool.

No answer.

Then McCool blew his nose and muttered, "Huh?" And suddenly he lunged out, his whole body lurching forward, to grab Julio's belt and slam him down. My body buckled, close to fainting, but in an instant Julio was laughing hysterically, while McCool wrestled him around, tickling and shouting, "Hit me!" and Julio pounded him and pulled his face, put his hand inside his mouth, felt his teeth, yanked it out, ran his hand over McCool's eyes roughly, feeling the bones, then his temples, his ears, which he pulled out and down roughly the way a baby might, and thrashed around with McCool now on his back, passive, allowing himself to be pummeled and explored, arms out and eyes shut.

This was an old familiar scene. I stood back and waited till it was done… like burning water, in place.

12-6

Tom arrived soon after the game was over, unshaven and wet, and Julio fell forward, burying his face in his overcoat, and wrapping his arms around him, asked him to stay. Tom – astonished – distracted – didn't lift his hands from his pockets but stared at McCool on his back on the floor.

A few speckles of gold paint still shone in his hair. He hoisted himself to his feet, asking, "Who the hell is this?"

"He's a monk," I said, "so be good."

I drew Tom into the kitchen and said, "I want you to get rid of him."

"Who?"

"McCool, that man, the Bumper."

"How?" asked Tom, his face drawn back in horror.

"Put him on a plane, Southwest, to the border. Let him have that place down there, just get him away."

"Do I have to go with him?"

"No, just put him on the plane at ten. A red-eye. It stops in Phoenix. I have the ticket."

"Oh, just take him to the airport?"

"Right, in a cab."

From the door Julio said, "I'm going too."

"What, why? You have to stay with me," I said. I grabbed and held a wet kitchen towel over my face to cool my eyes and whispered into Julio's hair: "Okay, go with them, honey. But Tom will bring you back here after the airport. You have school tomorrow." For the first time ever, Tom put his hand on me, telling me to calm down, he would bring

Julio home. I know that there were actions blind and rushed then, through bags and pockets and drawers, but they all seemed to bounce out of sequence like something solid spilling into parts. I called a cab and they all wore coats and carried keys. McCool had a backpack.

"What will I do down there on the border?" he roared. "It's the middle of fucking nowhere."
"Fix it up and watch your language. A child, a monk….Fix it up. Make it into something. You love that place so go!"
"I want to go to Ireland!"
"Too bad. Ireland doesn't want you."
He jumped towards me, and Tom hauled him by the back of his coat out the door, with Julio still clinging to his coat.
"You'll never see me again," were McCool's parting words called back to me from the elevator.

I ran to the window to watch. When I opened it up, icy rain floated across my face, and I leaned out so far the sill bit into my waist.

I saw the three of them, climbing inside a yellow cab, but McCool looked up at me, his face contorted like a tight fist. "Ma!" he called. "Don't make me go! Ma?"

12-7

For at least an hour I lay flat on my back waiting. Once I inspected the closet again, to see the wonder of McCool's creations, those figures and faces painted so meticulously according to some iconographic rules he must have learned somewhere. There was a figure, dark, with arms outstretched, who had silver and gold lines in his clothes and cheeks. McCool might say that this was his farewell and I would never see him again, but I didn't believe it. Instead I began to plan a move for myself and Julio—somewhere where we would live without him knowing, somewhere utopian, humane and gentle. But a great underlying sluggishness pulled at my ideas dragging them down as if they had too much water in them. I was afraid of McCool who had done the worst that could be done. Afraid of him at the airport, afraid of him at the border, afraid of him returning to find me, afraid of him coming for me when I was once again alone.

Exactly ten years before, during a premature blizzard, I left all my children at home and went to meet my best friends in the Hotel Commander. I did so carrying the weight of my husband like a tree on my back. This was a meeting I couldn't miss, no matter how low I stooped. The walk from the subway to the hotel was bitter, wet and shiny, just like this night. Traffic lights moved slowly on my right, while the brick walls and cold gray trees sopped up the gathering snow. I kept my eyes fixed on the left where dark areas behind shrubs and gates could conceal a man, and stepped up my pace. Lewis and Libby were already seated in a booth in a downstairs lounge, and later that night we would take a drunken walk up a white suburban hill, talking of group suicide and friendship. We made a deal. Then the two of them moved slightly off to the side, away from me, and their faces bluish from the snow light never looked more radiant to me. Lewis said, "Poor Henny. She knows when she is happy." "Maybe that's why she's so quiet."

Now it was nearly nine when I heard someone coming down the hall and opening the door. I was lying on my bed and closed my eyes, waiting for the worst. But Julio called me: "Ma!" I called back and he moved feelingly towards the bed and lay down there beside me, his cheeks rosy and cold.

Tom stood at the door and said, "Well, it's done. He's gone. Meek as a lamb once you were out of sight."

"Thank God for that," I said.

"So now," Tom announced, "I'll go."

Julio asked: "Till when? When will you come back?"

"Tomorrow–briefly–I'll see you off to school."

"Then why don't you sleep here? On the couch?" Julio asked.

"Scared the Bumper will come back?" Tom laughed. His face was bewildered, nervous, as he glanced around himself. "No."

"Then what?"

"I just don't want you to go."

I pulled off Julio's shoes and socks and got him his pajamas to put on, while Tom reluctantly unpeeled his coat and muttered that he might as well sleep over, if he was coming back anyway. I slapped out some sheets and laid out a quilt on the sofa, invented a pillow and sat on top of them all to test them. Tom stood awkwardly watching, his coat on his arm.

"Now what's wrong?" I asked him. "You've changed your mind?"

"No, no."

"So make yourself at home... Thank you... And goodnight."

I jumped to my feet, Tom took my hand as if to shake it formally, but instead he held it in both of his, and said, "I have changed my mind actually."

"Typical. You want to go home, then leave for Canada tomorrow, right?"

"No. None of that. I think I've decided. It's better. For me, for him, for Julio, for me to stay with you. For us to just keep on going. Together, I mean. Don't you think? I mean, what's the point in seeking meaning, so to speak, when this is what we have here? This child? I mean, something has to have meaning. And it would be a corporal act of mercy—like visiting prisoners, or the sick."

"Really?"

"That's what I think, I mean."

"Or think you mean."

"Right."

"Tom, don't worry. You continue the way you were going. We'll be fine."

"I thought you'd be glad!" he protested.

"I'm glad you thought of it, and meant it. But no, go, or sleep, then go."

"The Buddhist Dogen once told a story about a monk asking

his old master what to do when hundreds of myriad objects come all at once. And the master answered, Just don't try to control them," Tom said to me with a knowing smile. But I had plugged my ears with my fingers while he was talking and could barely hear the words. "Did you hear me? What do you think it means? No answer?" A long pause and then —"Okay, I'll sleep, then go," he assented, his face morose and shaded with a kind of apprehension that involved leaving me. "You sleep too, you've been through a lot."

"You go first."

"Don't worry. I won't look. Good night."

"Good night, Henny."

I went into my room, fell on the bed hard and rolled up beside Julio under the covers. Our feet were as cold as charity. He asked what was wrong. "Nothing, just tired."

He felt my face with the palm of his hand and brushed my hair back from my forehead. Then he rested his hand in the nape of my neck, as he always did when I told him a goodnight story. "You feel okay," he said. "Will you tell me a story?"

"Well. Now, okay.... This is an old, old one. Native American. I remember it was an old woman who told it to me when I was just a little girl. I slept in her bed for a few months and she told me stories, and strangely this is the one I remember from then."

"Go on, Ma."

"Once upon a time the sun was cheerfully burning in the sky and lighting up the world for everybody as usual. In those days the sun shone all the time, and there was no night. But suddenly the poor sun started to fall, spinning in flames, down, down onto the earth. It burned harder and harder but got smaller and smaller–until it became a tiny little human, a boy who was both weak and blind. He was like a little spark stuck inside of a person's bones. But he could no longer make everyone else see, the way he did when he was the sun. This upset him. Everything was scorched and brown around him, and the light was very dim.

"Meantime, nearby in a small village a big important chief was testing all the young warriors to discover one who would be a suitable husband for his beloved daughter. The warriors were all failures, one after the other. Either one was too greedy, or one was too drunk, or one was too funny, or one was too melancholy and one too mean–but whatever each one did, it ruined his chance at getting the girl to marry him. And at the same time the sky was ever-darkening, and the world seemed to be closing down for a very long and cold night. The people were scared, and the chief's daughter was especially upset because she couldn't see anyone she could love.

"At that moment the weak boy – the spark – wandered across the sand and out of the desert not knowing anything

SNEAK AWAY TO MEDITATE

about the contents going on. He stood and watched, with his mouth open, just the way you do. And I bet you can guess what happened. Yes. He – the poor sun, who had fallen to the ground – entered the contest and proved himself worthy! He really did. So of course the happy chief handed his even happier daughter to him right away.

"And at that moment the boy immediately grew huge and fiery and flared back into the sun in front of everyone's eyes and she, enflamed with love for him, became one with his fire and they melted and rose up into the sky together, filling the world with light and color again."

I watched the boy smile while he mused on the story, and then he said: "But you forgot something, Ma. What did he do to prove himself worthy?"

SEMIOTEXT(E) • NATIVE AGENTS SERIES

Chris Kraus, Editor

SEMIOTEXT(E) 2571 W. Fifth Street Los Angeles, Ca 90057
tel/fax 213.487.5204 www.semiotexte.org